PHANTASMAGORIA
Book 2:

DANSE MACABRE

by Trevor Kennedy

For Stephen Jones,
Best wishes,
Trevor.

COPYRIGHT INFORMATION:

Published in 2018 by
PHANTASMAGORIA PUBLISHING
through KDP

Dedicated to **John Gilbert**.

Thank you, my friend.

'The mind is its own place, and in itself can make a heaven of Hell, a hell of Heaven.'
(John Milton, *Paradise Lost*)

'Maybe this world is another planet's Hell.'
(Aldous Huxley, *Peter's Quotations: Ideas for Our Time*)

'Abandon hope all ye who enter here'
(Dante Alighieri, *Divine Comedy*)

CONTENTS

Notes:

Many thanks to **Jihane Mossalim** for her wonderful cover artwork and **Adrian Baldwin** for his amazing cover design.

The lyrics to *God Shuffled His Feet* are copyright of the Crash Test Dummies.

FOREWORD

By John Gilbert

All hope abandon, ye who enter here

*'O human race, born to fly upward, wherefore at a little wind
dost thou so fall?'*
(Dante Alighieri, *Divine Comedy*)

Gehenna is a valley just outside Jerusalem where the kings of
Judah sacrificed their children to huge fires. Those living in
the time of Roman occupations knew it as a cursed land, a
sprawling rubbish dump, where fires erupted like the leprous
pustules on the faces and limbs of the poor and sick who
survived on its meagre pickings.

It features in many of Jesus' parables and provides the
canvas upon which artists such as Hieronymus Bosch and
poets like Dante Alighieri and John Milton evoked their
visceral visions of infernal damnation.

For most, however, Hell is, as Stephen King's thaumaturge
Andre Linoge says in the television series *Storm Of The
Century*, repetition: repetition of circumstance, enslavement
to the cycles of substance abuse, addiction to negative
emotions such as hate and unrestrained rage or, perhaps most
common of all, day-to-day loneliness.

Many of those private Hells are explored in this, the second
collection of Trevor Kennedy's tales of terror, *Phantasmagoria*.
Indeed, in *La Muerte de la Humanidad*, he identifies Hell as
being, amongst other things, alone in an alien place. It is
separation from all that is familiar, all that we love and

perhaps even the God we worship or despise. The means by which this descent happens can be mundane or cosmic, mental, spiritual or physical.

In the case of *La Muerte*'s, the unnamed anti-hero, starts out in prison, a place which appears to be at the very borders of Hades, where the only route of escape from this place for its no-hoper inmates is heaped with the bodies of fellow inmates and demands the crossing of barriers of Styxian proportions. The reader might expect the narrative to end with the sweet relief of freedom, but all it means is transition into another vision of Hell, a dark barren landscape from which normal life has fled.

Many of the tales in this volume are written, like *La Muerte...*, as first person narratives. It is a natural choice for writers who want to sharply focus on the body at the centre of their tale, to show not only what they are seeing, hearing and feeling but also what they are thinking. It is a restrictive narrative viewpoint which doesn't allow reader - or writer - to wander, to escape what is being played out for us in graphic detail. And Trevor uses this sense of claustrophobic paranoia throughout this book. The title story, for instance, gives a whole new spin on disco inferno and swiftly develops into a banquet of the damned at a hotel that makes Stephen King's Overlook a kindergarten.

The Evil Men Do starts with an image of Hell as a state of mind, of depression, obsession in an post alcoholic haze brought into focus by a grim discovery and a realisation that nothing in life is certain no matter how innocent you may be now.

An Anagram of Funeral is Real Fun is something of a fragmented memory, of a revelation at a funeral from the corpse.

In *A Cacophony of Voices*, a mysterious envelope contains some very personal messages for the recipient, straight from Hell.

The Beast Beneath has resonances of the work of Chuck Palahniuk and Brett Easton Ellis as an essay in undisguised rage at the establishment. It descends into a maelstrom of anger and depression, as much a thirst for revenge as for alcohol, that gives birth to the world's real monsters.

One other influence on the nightmares you are about to experience is a real place, Northern Ireland, from where Trevor Kennedy hales. For many people who grew up in the UK, or indeed the US, in the 1970s or '80s, their view of Northern Ireland still percolates with pictures of violence, of blood and fire, bomb and bullet. But, Trevor grew up with intimate knowledge of what the media so fondly calls 'The Troubles' and lives there still. He knows the neighbourhoods, had a good, relatively normal, childhood amongst a kind and generous people and it is still his home. But, like any good writer, the land and its people inform his fiction, afford it scope and vision.

Trevor recently visited me here in Brighton where I met him face-to-face for the first time. In person he is a lively, funny, intelligent man who cares deeply about those around him. He runs a regular weekend radio show back home and has worked for the BBC. He has shown his talents not only in his stories but as the editor of *Phantasmagoria Magazine* he has a growing reputation in the horror and fantasy genres far beyond his home town.

His literary influences, however, are not bound to any one geographical place or time. They include the timeless deep horrors of Lovecraft and the depressed, demented tales of Poe, but they also reflect the shadowy social realism of James Joyce and and even E. M. Forster.

Like many authors, his writing is in part a form of release, of redemption. He pours his experiences and imaginings onto the page where it can be lived, vicariously, through the characters by the readers

Some may think he is lucky but I can understand why he is

such a good horror writer. Though, as I have just said, he tells me he had a happy childhood - I've seen the pictures - I also know that he has seen and experienced the dark side of life. He has that dark shard in his soul that I recognise in a kindred spirit. He's seen the brokenness of the world and yet survived: No, he has done more than that, he's done good. That's the mark of a special kind of writer; one who has been to Hell and back, as you're about to find out...

John Gilbert
Brighton, September 2018

PROLOGUE TO THE BOOK:

NO MORE BLUE TOMORROWS

So, there were these horrific-looking Muppet creatures doing Class A drugs all around me in some sort of weird factory setting with no exit. In the background, there was a lonely country singer with guitar, dressed in a comedy cowboy suit. He was crooning stereotypical sad songs about loneliness, depression, break-up, death, and all that sort of bleak shit. Although his song was largely unintelligible and distorted, I knew his story was one of a true, abject, and perfectly realised misery due to its sound, along with the man's general demeanour, his head drooped in a permanent state of despondency.

The Muppets themselves were nightmarish in appearance. Like some sort of denizen drones straight from the fiery pits of Hades itself. Their foam skin was dark blue, with greasy-looking, jet black curly hair spiralling from the sides of their bald heads. Aside from their bushy dark eyebrows, their faces were blank and expressionless, with no mouths and sunken black sockets where their eyes should have been, staring eternally into the void. I can't remember exactly what they were wearing but I think some of them may have had on the type of white lab coats you see government scientists in films wear. Their noses were pointed and big, but more like the sort of nose Count Von Count from *Sesame Street* has, as opposed to Gonzo, who is actually from outer space or something. These Muppet abominations were hoovering huge wads of cocaine up their nostrils and some were even cooking up and shooting H in sharp syringes too.

The gear they were taking like it was going out of fashion

must have been laced with some really dodgy shit - maybe rat poison or brick dust like the paramilitaries used to put in bad Es back in the 1990s - because all of a sudden they began OD-ing, almost in unison, as if choreographed by some sort of pretentious performance art dance teacher. Deep red blood pissed from their big Muppet noses and out of their tiny Muppet ears. Some of them trembled and shook violently, like they were taking extreme epileptic fits, shrieking high-pitched, deafening, screaming sounds before collapsing on the floor motionless, their cute little Muppet lab coats and all around them saturated in a dark crimson mess.

There was complete silence for a short while, maybe just a few seconds, before the seemingly unfazed country singer broke the monotony with a brand new, even more joylessly melancholic dismal refrain.

It is obvious to me now what these Muppets represented. I think we all know the true nature of their meaning.

THE DANSE MACABRE

*'And those who were seen dancing were thought to be insane
by those who could not hear the music.'*
(Friedrich Nietzche)

*'I don't believe you'd like it, you wouldn't like it here.
There ain't no entertainment and the judgements are
severe...'*
(Leonard Cohen)

As the three friends and workmates at Bombardier Shorts' Dunmurry plant finished work early on that Friday afternoon, none of them could have ever imagined the depraved horrors they would soon bear witness to over the coming weekend.

This is their story. A story so terrifyingly bizarre it could easily be written off as an unrealistic flight of fancy, but it is true, every single word of it. A tale of creatures who walk by night, humanity at its most reprobate, and the Great Blue Beast which shall rise again for the final time with a howling, screeching insanity, ensnaring the light and screaming an eternal bellow from the ancient inferno below.

Part One: *DUNMURRY YOUTH CLUB*

June 2018

It was a pleasant summer's day and the aircraft manufacturers were making their way to the seaside resort of Shannon for a short golfing holiday. As Fiction Factory's *Feels Like Heaven* blasted from the car radio, composite operators

Paul McBride, Davy Jones (he'd heard all The Monkees jokes many times before, you know) and Stumpy made their way from the aerospace factory on the outskirts of South Belfast and onto the M2 motorway, bound for the tranquil little holiday haven that is Shannon, for a few rounds of golf and alcoholic beverages. Paul was their pilot in his dark green Vauxhall Astra, Davy the cheerful co-pilot, singing along badly to the tunes, and Stumpy in the back cracking the jokes. Sadly, work jester and teller of tall tales, the legendary Whizz, couldn't make it, obviously off on one or more of his made-up sexual conquests again, the randy old devil that he was. The golf clubs were locked safely in the boot, the windows down, the blistering sun shining marvellously down from the cloudless heavens above, putting the boys in a very light-hearted and jovial mood indeed, with the real fun just about to begin. It was bliss. Happy days were here again, it seemed.

The buddies had been working together as part of the same team (a squad consisting of around thirty bodies, mostly men, but some women, operating a day and night shift between them, four weeks about) in the firm for over four years together, their place of employment being the well-reputed and respected aircraft manufacturers founded in 1908 by the Short brothers, the first company in the world to ever design and make production aircraft parts, with other notable achievements by 'Shorts' being a highly recognised contribution to the Allied war efforts during the first and second world wars, and their 'flying boats' of the 1950s. Still to this day providing plane components, engine nachelles and flight control systems with great efficiency and high standards around the globe, and employing a few thousand men and women in their various factories scattered across the country, the golfing holiday makers were part of a workplace body which cut, measured and laid up materials such as Kevlar (the stuff the police bullet proof jackets are made of) and fibre glass for the company's Regional Jet contract. In the past, they had also collectively plied their talents for the Boeing, Global and Learjet squads there.

The work itself was not that difficult, tricky or time-consuming, so on a daily basis they enjoyed the cheeky pleasures of extended smoke and coffee breaks, chess and card games on the much quieter night shift (with only one manager, old Billy McMillan, on duty in the evening, it was a lot easier to get away with), and plenty of frolicking and messing around, including the rather offbeat biscuit eating competitions and chair races. By the way, an employee known to all as simply Fish won the biscuit eating competition that year, although he did have to suffer the indignity of having his cup of tea spiked with laxatives during it.

For a presumed place of lashings of toil and sweat, they really did have some good times and laughs together over the years whilst employed there, with a great after-work social scene prevalent also. The place would often be affectionately referred to as Dunmurry Youth Club, such was the enjoyment that was regularly had. With strong unions, camaraderie and an excellent rate of pay, it made things all the sweeter. Some of the line managers could be real ball busters at times, however, but one just simply learned to take the rough with the smooth and overall it was a fine place to endure the daily grind, especially considering the more less attractive working class jobs out there, such as call centres and cheap gruelling manual labour on building sites.

Golf has always really been the past-time of middle-aged men now past their physical best, a borderline tedious hobby for many, but one that can be gradually adjusted to, I suppose, with the post-game drinks being the main highlight of the whole set-up really. Now in their forties, the three friends had adapted well to this relatively new interest for them.

Paul glided his almost camouflage-coloured vehicle gently into the tidy car-park of the grand in scale Shannon Golf Links Hotel, while Nik Kershaw was crooning something about not letting the sun go down on him from the airwaves. They had been listening to some new radio station based in Newtownards named Big Hits Radio UK, which seemed to specialise in playing retro music from the 1970s and 1980s. It did indeed play some great sounds, but the presenter, it had to be said, was somewhat annoying in his over-enthusiasm for said eras.

The hotel was connected to the infamous Xanadu nightclub, which operated from the side adjoining building. Infamous due to its highly liberal attitude to illegal drug use within its sleazy walls, the place being a bit of a well-known den of iniquity in the 1990s for young Ecstasy-fuelled ravers dancing the nights away and undesirable criminal types peddling their illicit gear to the loved-up youths of the time. There had also been a widely-reported unsolved double murder in the surrounding woodland in 2003. A couple of girls in their early twenties had inexplicably disappeared from the nearby caravan park where they had been staying during the Easter period that year. Extensive and worried search parties of police, locals and their families drew nothing but blanks, but their bodies were eventually discovered in a bad way in the aforementioned woods, the fledgling ladies' corpses apparently, according to local witnesses, the victims in part to crude acts of violation, dismemberment and cannibalism. Which brings us nicely to the rumours of witchcraft-related sorcery in the area, put down to old wives' tales by many. Over the years, local teenagers terrified each other with yarns of the hotel being built on the site of an ancient witches' burial ground, peopled by enchantresses who had been put to death by the good God-fearing people of centuries past. There was even the odd belief that no birdsong or natural life could be experienced at certain parts of the forestry. All this and other apparent silliness. None of it has ever been scientifically proven, of course.

The posse of three were greeted at the hotel by an elderly, yet charismatic lady with long wavy grey locks and deep emerald eyes, which looked as if they had experienced many great and interesting sights throughout a life well lived. She wore a flowing hippie-style red dress, which almost matched the magenta wallpaper of the recently refurbished lodging. The place may have been modernisned to nice effect, but it still retained a certain charming retrospective feel about it, witnessed in the furniture and 1930s art deco stylings. Visible on the right was another rather grand and spacious room with an old-fashioned open fire, it being unlit due to the still reasonably hot late June afternoon, but at the same time still an inviting centrepiece to the stylish wooden bar, also part of this club house next to the lobby where the would-be golfers were at. Although they had never checked up on it, the hotel probably had a three star rating from whichever body it is that makes those sorts of decisions.

The original building was Victorian in manner, it first being erected as a restaurant when Queen Victoria was still enjoying the early years of her reign on the throne. It was an eating establishment and meeting place for the rich and well-to-do back then. Over the years, the Victorian design had given way to various updatings and extensions, including the adding of the nightclub, but much of the old original look could still be found and felt inside if you looked hard enough in the right places.

The eccentrically fascinating old woman, who introduced herself confidently as Mrs McDonagh, regaled them with small-talk narrations about how her hotel was a family-run business and had been since the 1960s when herself and her dear husband, Thomas, had bought it over and essentially saved it from ruin and abandonment. The perceived insane previous owner had let it go to the metaphorical dogs, almost allowing it to fall apart and collapse around him. They redecorated and re-opened, and business was soon booming for the new-look Shannon Golf Links. The nightclub and golf course just across the road were unveiled proudly together in 1976, and they became just another couple of big attractions for holidaying families and friends on well-earned breaks to the much-loved town of Shannon, which was just one mile down the main road that ran through it, and also included the beauteous sand dunes of the golden beach and, of course, Larry's Amusement Arcade in the town centre. Some of the highlights of Larry's were, for most of the kids and big kids anyway, the big dipper, ghost train and dodgems.

The strangely intriguing Mrs McDonagh enlightened the men that her other half was having an afternoon nap and her grown up twin sons were just readying their rooms, so if they would wait in the club house the rooms would be ready within the hour, adding that they could look forward to an appetising breakfast in the morning. The guys politely acknowledged and agreed, re-slung their bags and clubs over their shoulders and entered the bar.

A young raven-haired slight woman serving the drinks behind the counter made herself known as Leanne in a thick east-Antrim accent, probably a Larne one at that, and set the Belfast travellers up with a pint of Carlsberg each, which Davy paid for with his credit card. To the left of the bar, a tall, slim and fair-haired man in his mid-to-late thirties was very drunkenly dancing along to Cyndi Lauper's *Girls Just Want To Have Fun*, which was loudly emitting from the jukebox just to the right of the centre fireplace facing the bar. What was it with this trip and 1980s pop music anyway, Paul thought to himself as Stumpy and Davy grabbed a table and some seats. The drunk man was sweating profusely due to his ridiculous, but committed, dance moves and the dark bags under his bloodshot eyes suggested he hadn't slept properly for days, maybe even weeks, and may have been drinking heavily or taking some form of drugs for a similar period. As the pals took their seats beside the fireplace and jukebox, he clocked them and stopped dancing, soon awkwardly staggering in their direction accompanied with his half-empty (or half-full, depending on your outlook on life, but Drunk Man was almost certainly a 'half-empty' sort of guy) pint bottle of Strongbow cider, which he was drinking from straight, sat down at their table, obviously looking for new company to entertain and no doubt eventually become a major source of irritation to, and spoke in a crude, pissed up, though surprising coherent city accent:

"That's one of my favourite songs of all time, so it is. I fuckin' well love it and Cyndi Lauper was some piece of kit back in the day too. She probably still is, actually. She would definitely get it! I actually think she was better than Madonna back then. Do you ever see the state of Madonna these days? She's like some mad old woman trying to relive her youth. And Cher too? Fuck me, what's that all about? Nice to meet you anyway, lads. I'm the Bossman from Belfast. I came up here for a bit of a break and to sort my head out, but fell off the wagon a few days ago, fuck sake, and have been blocked ever since. I think the auld doll and auld lad who own this place are ready for kicking me out and they almost called the peelers for me the other night. I know I can be a wee bit loud when I'm on the sauce, but there's no real harm in me. Fuckin' nightmare though. What are yous doing up here anyway, lads?"

The Bossman, as drunkenly annoying as he could be, managed to wangle his way into the workmates' company, joining their drinking round and chatting away seemingly quite knowledgeably about subjects as diverse as sport, North Korea, 1970s cinema and American twentieth century history. They never did find out his real name.

The drinking session between the four men started well enough, with merriment-filled chatter concerning various topics ensuing. But Stumpy was taking a particular disliking to the Bossman, perturbed by his somewhat brass neck of crashing their party. The drunkard's general loudness and inebriated silliness - which included spilling an entire round of drinks, some of which splashed over Stumpy and Paul's trousers - was beginning to grind the workmates' gears, particularly Stumpy, who, as the drinks went down, was gradually getting more and more aggrieved with this wasted arsehole in front of him.

Please allow me if you will, at this point, to introduce you properly to the three workers and would-be golfers. The dark-haired, short in stature Stumpy was named so because of his misshapen right hand, which had been badly injured several times over the years in a series of unfortunate coincidental accidents which had resulted in him losing the tops of his middling fingers. When he was just eleven years old, whilst delivering Belfast Telegraph newspapers on his usual route for a local newsagent's shop in his native East Belfast district, one of the heavier letterboxes prematurely snapped down on his hand as he was posting a newspaper through it. This resulted in the severing of his middle finger and lots of blood splattering on the rest of the papers in the sack that day. At fifteen, during a riot in his area with a rival group from the 'other side', Stumpy lost the top of his ring finger thanks to a firework he was about to throw exploding too soon. It should be said though, back in the darker days of the Northern Ireland 'Troubles' the majority of rioting from all sides was more about protecting your area from attack, unlike the mainly recreational rioting of more contemporary times. Anyway, the other scars on his hand were due to a vicious dog attack when he was twenty-two. Still, none of this ever kept Stumpy back, who was a very fun-loving and witty fellow, if a little crazy with a touch repressed anger at times. He really didn't suffer fools lightly either and was married with five children.

The lanky, curly-haired Davy Jones, was also married with two children and was known for being a bit of a joker as well. An apparent master gambler, his winning streaks on the horses and footballing bets were fast becoming the stuff of legend, with many other would-be punters seeking his sage-like advice and tips.

The athletically built ex-fireman, Paul, was the sensible one of the bunch, no-nonsense and very much self-disciplined. He did enjoy letting his hair down at the weekends though, was a bit a fount of knowledge of all things relating to music - from the Beatles to the more modern day stuff - and hailed from the Shankill Road area of Belfast, where he shared his home with his long term partner and a couple of pet cats.

The drinks soon progressed from beers to spirits, as the

candour between the group grew more boisterous as the evening went on, the Bossman still tagging along, despite almost nodding off on several occasions, much to Stumpy's annoyance, who was beginning to act much more aggressively and was at this point looking to leave the bar, which now had quite a few other customers in it, and head next door to the Xanadu nightclub to get their hands on some Ecstasy pills, dance into the wee small hours and hopefully pull a few women and get them back to the rooms too. Davy suggested they ditch the Bossman and just turn in for the night as it was getting rather late already and they would be up early in the morning for a round of golf which would be ruined if they were too hungover. Paul, who was beginning to get more than a little tipsy, was up for Stumpy's idea of the nightclub and pills, and argued with Davy over this, things almost threatening to get a bit out of hand between the trio. The intoxicated Bossman (who incidentally wasn't actually the boss of anything, it was just his nickname), was oblivious to most things going on around him.

The men eventually agreed that they had all had a bit too much to drink and heading to their rooms to unpack and get to bed would probably be the best option for all, as they could always hit the nightclub on the Saturday night when it would be more livelier anyway. With the help of the hotel owner's rather blank-faced twin sons, who were now working behind the bar, they helped the barely conscious Bossman back to his room firstly, as he mumbled incoherently and angrily to himself. Out of badness, Stumpy hit him a few fly slaps around the head as they carried him to his cot.

After sorting out their belongings, the three men retired for the night, Stumpy in a single room and Davy and Paul in a shared room with twin beds.

Part Two: *THINGS THAT GO BUMP IN THE NIGHT*

BANG!

"The fuckin' electric's went out, fer fuck's sake!"

Davy and Paul jolted upright in their beds after the rude awakening from Stumpy.

"What the fuck are you playing at? What time is it?" enquired Davy whilst checking the light switches with no success.

"It's about half three in the morning. I can just about make out my watch in the moonlight from the window. The electric's went out in the whole place it seems and the phones in the rooms aren't working too. No mobile signal either, fuck sake," retorted an upset Stumpy.

The two men in bed got up and tried to get their eyes accustomed to the dark. Paul pulled back the blinds on the window above his bed. Outside the world seemed dead, or at very least sound asleep.

"We may head down to the reception and report it to that auld doll. See if she can get it sorted," stated a now more alert Paul.

"Ballix to that. I say we just go back to sleep and let the owners get it fixed in the morning. It's probably just a power cut affecting the general area," replied a still very tired Davy.

Without warning a tremor rumbled throughout the room, accompanied by a deafening banging from somewhere below, like that of a large animal stampeding. They were on the second floor, but this crashing appeared to be coming from deep within the hotel's foundations.

"What the fuck was that?!" exclaimed Stumpy.

"C'mon and we'll head down to the reception and find out from the old woman what exactly is going on here," demanded a worried Paul.

After Paul and Davy put on some clothes and the three men exited the bedroom, from underneath there came more thunderous crashing, causing the walls and floor around them to shudder. They made their way in the dark carefully down the stairs facing the bedroom, towards the reception area below, hardly making a sound between them apart from Paul's comment that it seemed strange that they were apparently the only guests wakened by the commotion. Davy pointed out that apart from the drunken Bossman from earlier, he didn't think there were many other guests staying, if any. There was a decent crowd in the bar and heading to the nightclub earlier, but none of them seemed to be boarding for the night.

At the bottom of the stairway, they took a left down a pitch black corridor, feeling their way down it, until they got to the reception area's door, a dim sleek of light emitting from its window, caused by some moonlight shining through inside from the interior window. But the door was locked and there was no-one inside the reception anyway. The main front entrance, which was at the very end of the corridor, was also bolted shut.

"What'll we do now, fer fuck's sake?" questioned a now rather exasperated Stumpy.

Paul replied, "I reckon we should go back upstairs to where we were and down that long corridor past your room, Stumpy. We might be able to get outside from the other end of the hotel, maybe even through the nightclub."

Stumpy and Davy agreed.

As the men felt their way back upstairs, there was more unsettling rumbling and shaking from below.

When they got to the top of the stairs, Paul took the lead but as he went to round the corner on the left he was greeted by a tall, dark, silent figure which collided into him, knocking him back into his two friends and causing the three of them to topple down a few stairs. When they composed themselves, an enraged Stumpy took a run towards the mysterious figure and reigned punches down on its head, it soon dropping to the ground.

"Ah, fuck. Ah, fuck. Stop hitting me. Stop hitting me. It's only me, fuck sake! The Bossman. I don't mean yous any harm."

On the realisation of who it was, Stumpy ceased his attack.

"What the fuck are you playing at, jumping out on us like that?" shouted Davy.

The Bossman appeared sober. "I didn't mean it, for fuck's sake. I can't see were I'm going. Something's wrong here. There's no other guests or staff and it sounds like there's an earthquake going on downstairs somewhere. It's knocked the electric off and I think we're locked in too."

"We're gonna try and get out of here through the other side where you just came from. Your room is near where the nightclub is, right?" asked Paul of the Bossman.

"Yea, the nightclub kicked out a while ago now so there's no-one about and it's near impossible to see where you're going."

"We'll just have to try our fuckin' best. Now c'mon, you lot," added Davy.

The four men clambered their way gradually through the new corridor, down some stairs on the right and onto another passageway which they reckoned would bring them close to the main nightclub arena. The loud shaking and noise from below continued sporadically, disturbing them all to great effect.

In the passageway they were now on, on the ground floor,

the men began to hear some faint music, gradually increasing in volume as they moved along. It was coming from a door at the very end of the hall. It was dance music. Indeed it was a particular sub-genre of club music known as deep trance, almost hypnotic in its strange electronic rhythmic sound, like some sort of coded otherworldly communication from another universe altogether. *Follow me, follow me...* the music whispered in their ears in its alien voice, getting louder and louder for each step they took.

Follow me, follow me...

They reached the door where the strange music was coming from. Paul turned the handle and it opened up, revealing the most beautifully lit dance floor imaginable. It was almost dreamlike, as if the empty floor was filled with the aurora of diamonds and the essence of the sharp glowing bright colours ahead - vivid purples, blues, greens and golden rays - that shone and collided with all around it, as the unearthly voice begged them once again to *Follow me, follow me...* in perfect harmony with the trance beats it was a part of. The four men entered the room in silence, one after each other, and walked to the centre of the dance floor, transfixed somewhat, looking all around them in awe at the mystical light show on display in front of their very eyes. It was as if they had somehow been removed from time and space itself.

Suddenly the music stopped dead.

Silence for a brief period. And then a new tune came on, seemingly from out of nowhere, but filling the arena with a pumping soundtrack. Stumpy spoke up:

"I know this one, hahaha. It's called Wizards of the Sonic or something. The Red Jerry mix by an outfit called Westbam. It's an old one from the early 1990s, from back in my younger raving days, haha."

"I recognise it as well, and the last one," muttered the

Bossman.

"Yea, me too, mate, they're both club classics from the nineties," responded Stumpy before adding, "Sorry about hitting you earlier, big lad. Didn't mean it. You just jumped out on us like that and I hadn't a clue who you were."

"Don't worry about it, pal. No biggie. I've received worse beatings than that over the years."

"There's some extremely weird shit going on here tonight. I don't like it. What the hell's going on?" a perturbed Davy offered.

But the extremely weird shit he spoke of was just about to get increasingly weirder, as from beyond the shadows, out of the corners of the large room, as if slithering out from the very cracks of the walls themselves, came a horde of bodies, moving disjointedly to the timing of the rave music to surround and fixate malevolently on the four innocent souls gathered at the centre of the dance floor. Horrible, degenerate, deplorable creatures - ghouls, if you like - monsters that exist in those twilight realms of existence. They were the phantoms of long-dead revellers from over the years at Xanadu, souls claimed by a menacing, eternal evil that had long resided in the place.

The ghouls were attempting to dance to the music, a bizarre sight, their rotting faces bloodied and clothes tattered. One of them, a female, was wearing a blood-stained wedding dress and another carried a head on a spike. The rest were an assemblage of wretched puss and living death, covered in sores and boils, whilst emitting the most putrid of foul odours. Abominations from another plain, some crawling on the ground, they danced awkwardly around the four men as the music stepped up a gear towards the heightening crescendo of its first section, their faces intent on snarling devilment. And theirs was the dance of death - the danse macabre!

Paul, Davy, Stumpy and the Bossman were all frozen to the spot in pure terror and bewilderment, muted in their shock. It's was like some sort of clubbers' graveyard. As the music reached its melancholy synthesiser-based bridge section, the Bossman moved to the side and knelt down facing the other three men, his head in his hands, totally confused as to what was going on in front of him, trying to make some coherent sense of it all, but to no avail. One of the ghouls, wearing a dirtied and torn tuxedo, noticed him and crept slowly up behind with a razor sharp blade in hand, pulled the Bossman's head back violently by the hair and sliced his throat open, exposing the jugular section, with deep red pouring from it and hitting the floor with an uncomfortable splatting sound, just before his body slumped to the ground, jerking at first but eventually remaining motionless.

When the other men realised fully what was going on they instinctively panicked and one after the other made a run for it, breaking through the gathered monstrosities and towards the door at the other end of the large room. The Bossman was dead and there was nothing they could do about that fact now.

They escaped into a hallway which contained stairs leading downwards again, this time seemingly underground. As they dashed down the stairwell, everywhere around was shaken nosily by whatever it was that occupied the space far below this nightmarish hotel.

Down the stairs led to another corridor, but this one was lit with black candles in candlesticks hanging from the walls. It ended in a dead end, but there were two doors within, one on the near left and another to the far right. The friends argued with raised emotional voices about what exactly was happening in this unreal situation, how they should proceed, and where they could raise the alarm. Still no mobile phone signal. Each of them was profoundly frightened and affected by the horrors they had just witnessed, now feeling trapped within the walls of the hotel. They eventually decided upon looking to see where the first door on the left would lead them to. It led to another room which had the word *Forneus* etched on its wooden entrance.

Death filled the air once again. The scene in front of the work colleagues was one of chaotic, twisted imagery. Blood was everywhere, strewn across the floor and walls, as were body parts - some animal, some evidently human in origin. A place of unholy consternation - bones, mess and other debris were littered all around. A Satanic altar stood at the centre of the back of the room, complete with black candles, talismans and a sinister-looking grimoire with a human skull resting upon it. Above the altar, on the wall was a very detailed painting. The artwork was impeccable. On it was displayed a beautiful, yet grotesque image of a large beast, with the body of a voluptuous woman and the head of a leopard. Its skin was blue and scaly, like that of a serpent's, with completely black eyes resting in its sockets. From its mouth, sharp fangs protruded and on the hands were deadly claws. Above the chilling painting was a message, written in dripping blood:

The Great Blue Beast shall rise from the neverending sea of human filth and hatred, devouring all around her. And those insignificant weaklings of mankind who remain shall bow down and worship her majesty. But this is only the beginning of the final days. The eternal dark times and second death of the human race will be splendidly terrifying in its execution.

Simply looking upon the face of She, who is also known as Wormwood, shall drive them insane, as they rip each other from limb to limb. And the great whore of temptation, the bringer of eternal pain shall be pleased.

Paul, Davy and Stumpy looked on, stunned, as an aroma entered the room, a rather pleasant perfume-esque scent, filling the air inside. Before they could properly take in the spectacle in front of them and the sweet whiff in the air, they noticed a sudden movement from under the altar.

A small, demonic-looking, red-skinned figure, about the size of small child, complete with tail, deformed head, contorted face and forked tongue darting in and out of its ugly mouth, bolted across the room towards them, specifically in the direction of Stumpy and pounced on him, sinking its sharp teeth into his balls. He screeched in agony, as his friends looked on aghast, perplexed trauma etched on their faces. Blood seeped through Stumpy's jeans from his crotch area, just as he collapsed onto the ground unconscious. The creature took one final lunging bite into his groin before escaping hastily back under the altar at the far side of the room. Just as Paul and Davy were about to do something to help their friend, the fumes of the pleasant fragrance overcame them, resulting in them passing out also and dropping to the ground.

Part Three: *RED DINNER*

The table was set. The meal prepared.

Paul could hear muffled sounds and voices, both male and female, speaking but everything around him was still in darkness.

"Is he awake yet?"

"What shall we do with this one?"

"The same as the others, I suppose."

"Come on, breakfast is being served..."

Paul eventually regained proper consciousness, still dizzied and confused, however, but taking in all around him, despite being tied with rope firmly to a wooden chair by his hands and feet which were now shoeless. His head throbbed in agony. He ached all over and felt so nauseous he thought he was going to vomit.

In front of him was a grand and spacious room. A dining room. Shutters covered the windows of the richly papered dark purple walls to his left. Similarly-coloured thick velvet curtains hung proudly, whilst the freshly mopped stone black floor glistened somewhat.

Although seated slightly away from it, Paul turned his attention to the elegant, stretching dining table facing him. It was peopled by four diners. The elderly female owner of the hotel from before at the bottom, a brutish-looking balding older man, presumably her husband, at the top, and their gaunt, expressionless twin sons at the near centre.

The table itself was decorated in a black table cloth, with the seemingly blacker candles in their candlestick holders producing the only light in this sinister room.

On a large silver tray were crude cuts of freshly cooked meat - apparent legs being the most recognisable - readied for consumption from the family's best china and cutlery situated at each place on the table. But there was a certain detail Paul couldn't really make sense of at first, almost as if his brain had failed to properly register it upon originally taking it in - a reflex safe setting perhaps - the grand centrepiece of the epic dinner table was three newly severed human heads on a platter - their mouths still slightly agape, frozen in terror - the decapitated heads of none other than Davy, Stumpy and the Bossman!

A terrified Paul began to wretch and struggled to get free but to no avail, the noise attracting the alerted attention of the McDonagh family.

"Our friend has awakened. What will we do with him now, father?" asked one of the twin sons.

"Don't let him bother you, Cain. He can do us no harm in his current situation. Just enjoy your breakfast and we can have the pleasure of his company later on for dinner," replied the father, Thomas.

"If he becomes too troublesome, you and your brother will have to deal with him. Now, enough talk. Relax and eat your meal before it goes cold. I didn't spend all that time preparing it in the kitchen for it to go to waste," added the mother, Mrs McDonagh, calmly.

"Of course, mother. And thank you for sharing the livers with Abel and I. I know they are your favourites."

"Come on, son! To start the morning with a cooked meal for breakfast like this is a rarity, and will set you up for the rest of the day and keep you strong and healthy. Think of all that good protein!" a somewhat pleased with himself Thomas exclaimed before taking a sip from his glass of freshly squeezed orange juice.

As Paul vomited on the floor in front of him, the family serenely passed the tray of human meat around, carving off chunks from the legs as one would do with a Christmas turkey perhaps, and placing them on their plates beside the fried eggs and mushrooms.

"Could you pass the brown sauce please, father," asked the pale-faced Abel as the family tucked into their nourishing meal.

Paul's sides were now crippled with pain from the vomiting. He was afraid and profoundly confused, like a tourist in an especially surreal nightmare. He knew he had to do something fast and racked his brain for ideas.

"I need to go to toilet." Paul's question stopped the family's eating of his friends dead in their tracks. They looked at each other with quizzical faces, taken aback slightly by the question. Eventually the father, Thomas, replied:

"Tough shit. You may hold it in. You're going nowhere, my friend."

"I'm not messing around here. I really need to go." There was a nervousness and desperation in Paul's voice.

"Is it for a piss just? If that's the case then you may just wet yourself. It's not important," chirped Mrs McDonagh callously.

"I need to go for a dump as well. If I shit myself here it will stink out the whole room and ruin your little dinner party. Not to mention the mess you would have to clean up too."

The family exchanged hesitant glances with each other. Abel broke the short silence:

"You can't let him go, mother. He'll try to escape and he's quite a well built man. We'd have real trouble trying to stop him and if he were to get away, then we'd be in all sorts of trouble."

Cain replied, "If it's managed properly we might be able to do it. This has never happened to us before."

"That's because we've never had as many guests together like this at the one time. It's usually only guests staying on their own we choose. Two at the most. I warned you all this could get out of hand very quickly. I thought it was a bad idea from the start," snapped the father.

Cain turned to Paul, "Do you really need to go or is this just some silly ploy to try and escape. You know, we'll fucking kill you there and then if you try any funny business."

"I'm telling you. I really need to go. I swear!"

Mrs McDonagh spoke next, "Okay, calm down, everyone. I think I know how to handle this. Abel and Cain, you go and get the butcher's knives from the kitchen. You then need to hold them right up against his throat on each side while your father unties him and escorts him to the toilet downstairs with him held firmly, arm up his back. The three of you are more than strong enough to handle him, but at all times keep the knives close to his throat and if there is any nonsense whatsoever, or even unexpected movements, push your blades deep into his neck, even when he's on the fucking pot! Now, let's get this over and done with. It's ruining my breakfast and I didn't slave away cooking it for all that time for nothing!"

The other family members agreed and the boys went to fetch the knives.

Thomas untied Paul slowly, watching his every move just as his sons were, their sharp weapons in place. Paul felt weak as a kitten as they frogmarched him cautiously out of the dining room and down some stone stairs to a corridor where the cold, basic bathroom was. Sunlight ebbed from the stained window above. It must have been around 7am, Paul pondered to himself as he considered screaming for help. But he decided not to, sticking to his original rather dubious plan instead.

Thomas ended the tense silence by commanding the orders to Paul, "Right. Listen carefully here. We go into this cubicle. Cain here will loosen your trousers and let them fall down. You step out of them and go to the toilet as quickly as humanly possible and in silence while both my boys keep their blades held to your throat. Any trouble at all from you and you will die a painful death from stabbing, then we will cut your dick off and eat you for dinner later on tonight. Do you agree?"

"Yes, I agree."

"You fucking better," snarled Cain, in an effort at further intimidation.

Paul knew his best, albeit highly dangerous, opportunity was fast approaching and it filled him with dread and a nervous energy.

Cain removed his knife from the right side of Paul's throat and nodded his head down marginally to begin removing his prisoner's trousers.

An adrenalin-fuelled Paul moved very quickly indeed, his strength heightened by blind panic and sheer survival instinct. He brought his knee swiftly up against Cain's face, shattering his nose with a thud and crunching of broken bones, blood spraying onto the floor. Abel immediately tried to cut Paul's throat, but the knife only partially entered as Paul snapped his head back, leaving a bad, but non-life threatening, gash. A powerful right-handed fist to the side of Abel's head caused him to fall back and slide down the wall of the tight space in the cubicle. Paul kicked behind him continually and wrestled with Thomas for a period, struggling hard in a frenzied determination not to lose the fight. Eventually an fierce elbow to the mouth did the job, with Thomas losing his grip on Paul and stumbling out of the small compacted space with a busted mouth. Paul then unleashed hell on the father, punching and kicking and gorging and biting for what seemed like a very long time indeed, full of a vengeful rage towards his captors, until in was clear that the bloodied mess in front of him was no longer breathing. He thrust down a final sweeping foot to Thomas's mashed up face, just to make sure. Paul turned his attention to the pathetic twins next, who were still lying in the cubicle stunned and nursing their wounds.

Now at the height of his extreme fit of vehement anger, Paul delivered vicious blow after blow on the heads of the brothers as they begged for mercy, but Paul was not really in any sort of forgiving mood that particular morning. He ceased briefly in his carnage to remove the old fashioned cast iron lid from the toilet cistern and hold it above Abel's cowering head, who was to be the first to receive the true retribution of his wrath. With an intense fury he did not know resided within him, Paul brought the heavy cistern lid down onto the head of the screaming Abel, crushing his skull and killing him outright. His brother's fate would follow presently.

Cain's arms flailed like a bird with broken wings as with a great velocity Paul sank the iron lid into the twin's head and decorated the cubicle surroundings with more red splatter and little chunks of brain and skull.

Paul stood in the bathroom, covered in the blood of his deserving victims but he knew this was not over yet. He had to deal with the old woman next and then get out of this wretched hotel and alert the relevant authorities as soon as possible. To say he had a bit of an incident to report to them was an understatement. He composed himself briefly before making a dash back up the stairs and into the dining room again.

As Paul opened the door of the impressive room and stood at it eyeing up Mrs McDonagh, who was still sat at the bottom of the table chewing on her macabre meal, she immediately turned around in her chair and with an energy unbecoming of a woman of her age, clenched her table knife firmly in her right hand and took a hysteric run towards him, screeching at the top of her voice like a banshee.

Paul simply stood his ground and as the maniacal woman frantically approached he kicked her hard in the chest before she had time to swing the knife. Her arms and thin body flew back wildly before colliding with the edge of the dining table, the left hand corner of it embedding itself deep into the back of her skull. And then she fell silent.

Gathering his bearings, Paul hurriedly left the room and dashed down through the corridors of the hotel before eventually finding himself once again at the reception area. With all his might he broke down the door and turned the place upside down before soon finding a bunch of keys in a desk drawer. He knew one of them had to open the front door of this detestable place. He then checked the pockets of his own jeans and was relieved to find his car keys still there. Those stupid bastards didn't even think of searching him and taking them from him, so sure they were he would never escape. It was time to check out of the Shannon Golf Links Hotel for good. A sliver of calm filled him for the first time in quite a while as he realised he had survived the night and the murderous intentions of the depraved family. His friends, Davy and Stumpy, and that annoying but generally good guy, the Bossman, had been butchered and eaten by them and he was going to have to do some serious explaining to their families and the police, but for now it was time to leave and get as far away as possible from this hell hole.

As the blood-drenched Paul left the hotel and into the early morning sunlight, he looked back briefly and tried to comprehend the unforgettable trauma and insanity he had just been through. Who would even believe such a crazy story? But the evidence was there within the hotel walls and he was sure his story would soon be headline news.

The sole survivor of this night of unimaginable mayhem got into his car and turned on the engine. The radio came on straight away. It was that irritating DJ from before again, who was now excitedly raving about the next song he was about to play. It was to be *She Drives Me Crazy* by the Fine Young

Cannibals.

Good song, but Paul really wasn't in the mood for it on this particular morning.

THE EVIL MEN DO: ANOTHER WARNING TO THE SELF-INDULGENT

'Here comes a candle to light you to bed,
And here comes a chopper to chop off your head.
Chip chop, chip chop...'
(*Oranges and Lemons*, traditional English nursery rhyme)

'What have I become, my sweetest friend?...'
(Nine Inch Nails)

There is a set of thick, majestic, jet black curtains which hang decadently in a strange and darkened room. On these curtains appear odd, indecipherable symbols etched in a white material. An ancient, long forgotten language? A coded form of communication by peculiar bodies of other astral plains? A forbidden tongue? No-one knows. And what lies beyond the curtains? The unseen monster - pure unadulterated evil and cruelty - and it is waiting patiently with baited breath.

This is in a world which cannot be found on any map. A place of unspeakable terror and undefined trauma. An area that exists only to torment and unleash unfounded pain and cruelty in every conceivable manner. Where the demons reside.

It is only on an extremely rare occasion one can break through this dimension and escape through the barriers in between worlds and behind the edge of consciousness wherein exists other realities.

The realm, this dark place, lies within the subconscious mind of Danny Madden.

***

I awaken. Not from the sleep of the innocent, but that of the guilty. Six straight days and nights of non-stop drinking have left me with a devastating feeling of impending doom. I know something bad has happened, something really bad. And this situation is only going to worsen greatly. I can't quite put my finger on exactly what this bad thing is yet, due to deeply clouded, confused memory banks, as blacked out as the darkest of winter nights. I need to go for a piss so badly my groin aches, but I cannot yet muster the energy to get up and relieve myself in the toilet. Maybe I should just let loose and piss all over the bed? It wouldn't be the first time.

I look around me. I am in the small bedroom of my two bedroom flat. Makes sense. I am naked with a dirty quilt pulled over me. The debris of the alcoholic binge fills my bedroom - empty vodka bottles, 'barrack busters' of cheap white cider, empty crisp packets, dried up spillages and cigarette burns on the long ruined wooden floor. Ash, feg butts seemingly everywhere. My portable TV has taken a fall off the table and onto the floor, probably now broken. When did that happen? My phone appears to be missing also but I'm sure it will turn up somewhere. It always does. There is a neat little pool of yellow vomit in the left hand corner of the room beside the door. Blood too. The same blood apparently that has leaked onto my mattress. Where the fuck did that come from? There is other mess, but I'm sure you get the general picture.

I roll over in the bed and close my eyes, wishing for sleep. When you're depressed as fuck with a big spoonful of paranoia and anxiety thrown in for good measure, all you want to do is sleep, for a very long time, in the vain hope that when you eventually wake up everything will be different and nice again. Like it was before, now a very long time ago indeed. I need a drink of water badly too. My mouth and throat are dry and raw.

I feel nauseous. I don't think I want to die, no, I'm too afraid to die right now, but I want God to take me away from this awful situation. It is too much to bear. I hate myself. I want to cry but cannot. I lie like this for minutes, maybe hours, maybe even days. Every time I drink or take drugs now it takes away a little bit of my soul that can no longer be replaced.

The hangover horn is now upon me. I imagine large naked, milky white breasts bouncing over me as I am being ridden by some unknown twenty year old nymphomaniac blonde slut. The thought passes and soon returns to the insidious fear and my aching crotch and dry-as-the-Sahara-desert throat. I really need water and to relieve myself badly but I am still too weak and scared to get up. I am existing in my own personal Hell and I am absolutely certain the Devil is waiting for me just around the corner, ready to pounce and claim his new and sweet-tasting fresh soul. A soul that was sold to him and the bottle almost twenty-five years ago now. It won't be long now, I reckon.

There is no more drink left in the flat. I have a memory of desperately running out of my poison before I eventually fell into a drunken coma last night. I remember frantically phoning around all the taxi places late at night, after the off licences and bars had closed, looking to see if any of them had any drink they could deliver, anything really. At least one of them told me to fuck off directly and another let me know that I was barred from their depot for life because I still owe them money for drink and for running off without paying a fare the other night. Another incident which I cannot recall.

I hate this world. Such a violent, nasty and unforgiving place. On this planet there are babies born with incurable, terminal illness, thousands of people are massacred on a whim daily for some petty squabble or another and thousands more starve to death, all the while as the great and the good turn a blind eye and either pretend they didn't see it or try to work out an angle with which it will benefit themselves. We've all seen those ghoulish teatime adverts, after all. What sort of a loving god would allow such misery to not just exist, but to thrive? More like an impotent or non-existent deity, if you ask me. Sometimes I just wish Putin or Trump or Kimmy or whoever would push that big red button and put an end to this wretched stink once and for all. I once heard it said that we would fail to evolve as a species if we did not have our struggles, but fuck me, give me a break please. Give us all a break, in fact. Even for the day. Just one day, that's all I ask.

I decide I will get up to relieve myself. Struggling to stand up straight, my head thumps as if there is someone banging on a Lambeg drum within. I stumble and almost fall, using the wall to steady myself. I put my hands over my face to try and bring myself around a bit. It is then when I feel the beard I now have after almost a week of not shaving. My teeth feel dirty and my breath stinks. I rustle my hair and its touch is greasy with little bits of dry skin and other detritus falling from it. I open the door and look at the landing and bathroom ahead of me. What appears to be an almost half full plastic bottle of Frosty Jack's strong white cider is propped up against the side of the door. I don't remember noticing it before, but it may come in handy very soon.

As I walk from the bedroom to the bathroom, I notice out of the corner of my left eye something which makes me stop dead in tracks. A wave of shock hits me first, followed by that horrible feeling of terrible realisation and memory returned. That one that reaches right into the pit of your stomach and rips out your innards. I turn and look into the open door of the main bedroom of my flat, beside the one that I just woke up in, and terrifyingly glare, mouth agape whilst beginning to shake all over, at a real life horror show I have created, one which I designed mere hours earlier before ringing those taxis depots in sheer desperation for more alcohol to take away the pain, or at very least numb it for a little while.

It is the dead body of the woman from last night.

I fall on the ground below and curl up into a little ball like I used to do as a small child. I cry loudly and punch the floor while begging God to make everything okay again, to give me a second chance, to make this horrifying event go away. I lie in this pathetic state of my own making for quite some time before calming down a little.

A thought comes. Maybe she's not really dead, but just unconscious or even sleeping? I jump up quickly and dash into the room and shake her body, pleading with her to wake up, begging her, desperately shaking and shaking and shaking this lifeless lump of meat, but all to no avail.

She is not sleeping or in a coma. She is a corpse, as dead as the proverbial Dodo. Her naked body is cold to the touch. She smells a little foul already and there are scrapes and bruisings all over her, especially on her throat and face where she is sporting two black, swollen eyes, the side-effect of a freshly broken nose, reminding me of a macabre version of Robert De Niro towards the end of *Raging Bull*. I eventually realise the futility of my efforts and gently place her back on the bed and pull a quilt over her body and head. I exit the room, now practically overcome with shock and fear and go back into the other bedroom and lie down on the bed and think, piecing together the previous night's events and what my plan of action should be next.

Her name is...was...Sharon, twenty-one years old. Or so she told me. She was a prostitute, a lady of the night I had hired for a couple of hours after getting her number from some sleazy website I had looked up on my phone. As soon as she appeared at my flat she wouldn't shut up, bitching and whining about the state of the place and the mess I was in myself. Constantly fuckin' nagging like an old fish wife and poking fun at my appearance too, making me feel even more badly about myself than I already did.

We soon had protected sex and it wasn't exactly classic stuff either. I came rather quickly and when I did Sharon got up and said that was it over for me and she was leaving. I said I had paid her for two hours service and she had to stay until those two hours were up, but she told me that once you come that is it finished and it was just tough shit for me. I pathetically begged her to stay, even for an hour. She was unrelenting. We argued. She lost her temper and began slapping and punching me. In turn, I went into a rage and punched her viciously around the head several times. She fell back on the bed and I pounced on top of her body, the both of us still as naked as the day we were born, and squeezed her throat extremely tightly while she kicked and flailed around in a panicked state. I kept hold of her throat in this same tightened grip until her kicking and shaking and wild movements stopped for good. And then I let go and went to fetch myself another drink.

What am I going to do? In a lifetime of terrible things happening to me when I was drunk this was without doubt the worst of the lot. In fact, stating it is the worst of the lot is more than an understatement. I have killed someone. I am a murderer now. A killer who has cruelly robbed a young woman of her life. So what if she was a prostitute. She was still someone's daughter, a daughter whose family would soon notice her missing and come looking for her. Along with the police eventually too, no doubt about it. I lie on my bed shaking and in some sort of heightened state of fear and shock, terrified at what I have done and what the repercussions of my vile act will be. I curse God for allowing this to happen and turning me into a lowlife alcoholic addict killer. I never wanted this sort of life! Why me?! I had promise, good jobs, happy relationships, and then alcohol came along and robbed me of it all. I don't deserve this and neither did that girl Sharon. It's not fuckin' fair! I want to die along with the girl but I'm too fuckin' cowardly to do it myself.

I'm going to have to hand myself in. There's nothing else for it. I will just be completely honest with the police and hope that the courts will have some mercy on me. I'll go to jail for a very long time, that's a certainty, but maybe, just maybe, something good will come of it one day. At least I will be sober in jail and no harm to anyone including myself. I'll do it. I'll find my phone and contact the peelers. But not yet, not just yet. Before I call them I need a drink. One final session before it is all over for me and they take me away.

I get up and storm out onto the landing and grab the half-finished bottle of Frosty Jack's and chug several gulps down my neck, some of it spilling down my chest. I need to put some clothes on. I go back to the small bedroom and hoke through the mess until I find boxer shorts and a t-shirt. After putting them on I go to the toilet and relieve myself, which, after I am finished, along with the effects of the cider beginning to take hold, calms me somewhat. I decide to shut the door to the bedroom where Sharon's remains are and go back to the other bedroom and finish the rest of this cheap and nasty bottle of cider. What time is it anyway? It must be around midday now and I'm going to have to find some smokes around this dump too, or at least retrieve some decent sized butts from the ashtrays.

After about an hour, I knock back the last of the cider and although I am feeling a lot more relaxed and clear-headed I am going to need more drink. I have a twenty pound note somewhere in the living room. I'll stick on a pair of jeans and trainers and once I find it I'll head to the off licence at the end of the street. I don't even give a fuck about my phone right now. I don't want to be in contact with anyone today anyway. When the time is right I will find it and then phone the police and confess my heinous crime.

The short walk to the off licence is a surreal one. I feel the passers-by are eyeing me up suspiciously, knowing full well that I have just committed some sort of unspeakable crime. It could just be my paranoia though and in all likelihood they are probably only staring at me because of the disgusting physical mess I am currently in. It's such a lovely day too, lunchtime on an early Saturday afternoon (I think its Saturday anyway). The sun is shining splendidly on this beautiful autumn's day and the shoppers are making their ways into town, as the crisp brown leaves litter the path ahead of me. Spring and summer are great, but surely autumn must be the most beautiful time of the year of them all. I'm going to miss enjoying little things like this when I get sent away, but it is the price I must pay for my terrible transgression.

I enter the wine lodge of sordid shame to make my filthy acquisition. The woman behind the counter, Anne, who knows me, looks me up and down and shakes her head in a combination of contempt and pity. I purchase another 'barrack buster' of Frosty Jack's white piss water, a litre of cheap vodka and a packet of cigarettes. I stare at the government health warning imprinted on the cigarette packet. The image vividly shows a man's open mouth with rotting yellowed and blackened teeth and huge blisters on his lips and gums. Above the picture it reads in large lettering, SMOKING CAUSES MOUTH AND THROAT CANCER. The image does not faze me in the slightest. In fact, it amuses me somewhat. I pay for my goods, exit the off licence and make my way back home. A funny-looking mongrel dog trots past me in the street and barks at me in a friendly manner. "Hello, dog," I reply to his silly yelps. It may be the shock of everything that has happened and most definitely related to the drink in my system, but a great calm has all of a sudden come over me. I am anticipating my final drink greatly before handing myself in and am now feeling almost accepting of my fate and what has went on in my house of horrors over the past few hours.

The drink slides down a treat. I drink the large bottle of cider first, over a few hours. I listen to music as I sit and think and look over my life so far. A life of missed opportunities and wastage. Nothing to show for it, except for lost chances, potential careers fucked up and meaningful relationships chucked in the bin. A pointless existence really. As a young lad I had it all in front of me, planned out. I was going to leave school at sixteen, move to the bright lights of London and become a fantasy artist just like my cousin, David. Whatever happened to that dream? It just sort of fazed out over my teenage years, soon forgotten about or put down to mere childish silliness. I was pretty good at illustrating too, but I haven't done it in many years now. Maybe I'll get back into it when I am in prison.

As I polish off the last of the vaguely apple-flavoured piss water, I fetch myself a beaker for the vodka which shall be downed straight, of course. The first beaker-full is a tough one to get down but I'm soon getting used to it. My mind drifts to other, more offbeat notions now. I don't really feel like going to jail today after all. If only that silly accident with the girl hadn't have happened. I don't deserve to go to jail. I didn't mean to kill her anyway. It was her fault for attacking me first, not to mention trying to rip me off in the first place. Like I say, an unfortunate accident. Could happen to anyone really.

But if it really was an accident, and I believe it was, then surely I don't deserve to go to jail at all, do I? The law will probably take a different view of events but if I am honest and cooperative with them then hopefully they will be sympathetic to my plight. Or maybe not.

What if I just don't tell anyone about the accident with poor Sharon and got rid of her body and any other incriminating evidence? I mean, no-one has come looking for her yet. Maybe she has no-one? Maybe no-one will even notice her absence? It's a long shot, but could be worth a try, for a greater good sort of thing, in that if I make a pact with God that after today I will live a completely sober life, stick close to Him and dedicate my life to helping others, he will protect me and keep my dark secret regarding Sharon safe from all prying eyes?...

Fuck it, I'll do it!

I grab some black bin liners from the kitchen and then run to the bedroom where Sharon's corpse is and begin searching through my old stuff. I toss photographs, dusty books and other nostalgic keepsakes out of their bags until I eventually come across the object I am looking for and the one which will aid me in my new plan - the old 'Rambo' knife that John Minnis gave me back in school in second form. It seems like

46

such a long time ago now.

I remove the quilt from Sharon's body and lift her up into my arms, feeling the coldness from her straight away and trying not to look at her messed up dead face. The drink has given me a renewed strength and determination. This will be a grisly affair but it has to be done and if I do it quickly enough it will soon be all over and I will be able to relax at last. I carry her into the bathroom and set her naked, motionless remains into the bathtub.

Armed with the 'Rambo' knife, which is not quite as sharp as I would like it to be, I get to work on the removal of her limbs and the bodily dismemberment ahead. I begin with the right arm. It really is tough going. The flesh itself is easy enough to get through, but the bone at the socket beside the shoulder blade is a real tough bastard and requires all of my strength and endurance, leaving me lashing with sweat. It leaves not as much mess as I first expected though, which I can only presumably put down to her blood having clotted quickly after death. I do still get the odd splatter over the good white bathroom tiles, onto the floor and over myself, however.

After a final pull and tug, the arm eventually comes free from my cutting and I fall back on the floor after it rips off in my hand. I'm out of breath due to all the hard work and decide to rest for a bit, before getting myself another beaker full of vodka and then working on the rest. If I can remove the other arm, legs and head then I can place them in black bags and dump them somewhere where nobody will find them, then work on cleaning this flat from top to bottom until it is spotless and an evidence free zone. I reckon there is no way in the world I could do this type of operation when sober, so I may as well make the most of the vodka and get it all over and done with as soon as humanly possibly.

After necking the beaker of vodka I decide to remove Sharon's head next, as I reckon the softness of the neck will be quite easy to get through with the knife. I dig in deep to her throat and move the knife around before effectively sawing off her cranium. As expected it comes off quite easily. Her decapitated head is a gruesome sight, the stuff of nightmares, so I try not to linger on it for too long and quickly put it into the black bag along with her arm.

I rest for a few seconds to catch my breath and then decide that Sharon's right leg should be next, as it is the closest to me. Then I will turn her over and remove the limbs from the other side. This is going to be a difficult one due to the obvious greater thickness of the leg bones and despite the massive effort and strength it will take, I just have to get this morbid sideshow done and dusted sooner rather than later, so I go to work on it with haste.

As before with the arm, I saw through the flesh of the upper thigh with ease, my knife gliding through the meat. It is as anticipated when I reach the bone, however, and my endurance of the sawing off of it requires my greatest strength yet. When I am about a quarter of a way through the job in hand, I suddenly feel a stiffness throughout my body, affecting, it appears, my muscles all over. I drop the knife in the bath beside the remains and fall back onto the bathroom floor in agony. My bladder and bowels give way involuntarily leaving a degrading mess all around me on the floor. I scream in pain as my body tightens and then convulses. The convulsions become violent and go on for what appears to be a long time, until they stop abruptly and I fall back onto the messy bathroom floor once again.

As my sanity and consciousness begin to slip away, I feel an enormous bolt of guilt rushing over me. I am so, so sorry for what I have done to that poor girl. If I survive this day I will most definitely confess all to the police when I hand myself over to them. I hate myself for what I have done. This is not me, not the real me anyway! This has been caused by the drunken waster within, the demon drink and all the Hell it brings with it. Please let me make amends, dear God. Please, I beseech you, one last chance! I'll do anything to put it right.

Anything at all! I'm sorry! I'm sorry! I'm sorry! I'm really, really sorry...

And then I slide out of awareness completely and everything fades to black...

***

I awaken with a massive jolt, leaping off my single bed like a jack-in-the-box. My white school shirt is soaking with sweat. Woah, that was fuckin' intense! I'm confused and entranced. Autumn sunlight seeps through the blinds covering my window. What time is it? I check the clock on my chest of drawers. It is situated beside a new macabre illustration I am working on. It's almost a quarter past four. Shit! I'm going to be late for my paper round.

I rush out of my room and am greeted by my mother bringing freshly ironed clothes into my sisters' room.

"Why didn't you wake me?!" I bark at her. "I'm going to be late getiin' down to the shop!"

"I was just coming up to waken you, son," she assures me. "When I came home from work at three you were sound asleep, completely conked out. What were you doing home from school so early anyway? Are you sick?"

"No, we got let out early for a teacher training day."

"You better not be lying to me."

"Mummy, I had this terrible nightmare that I was an old man in my forties and an alcoholic and I killed this woman. It all felt so realistic, like it was really happening."

"Ah, it was just a bad dream, son. Nothing to worry about, although maybe you shouldn't eat as much cheese as you always do, haha."

"It was terrifying. Really scary."

"Don't be silly. It was just a nightmare. We all have them from time-to-time. And you certainly don't look like you're in your forties either, haha. Fer flip sake, you haven't even turned thirteen yet!"

"What year is this, mummy?"

"Don't be daft!"

"Please, mummy. Just to put my mind at rest. What year is it?"

"That must have been some nightmare you had. It's 1989, of course. Now hurry up and get your papers delivered if you are going to make it to the Halloween disco at the leisure centre tonight."

"Thank you!"

And with that, I grab my bright orange paper bag and head for the newsagent's shop, still rather dazed from that horrific dream I just had. What was that all about? It was all just so graphic and gory. Definitely a really weird one. Maybe it was a premonition of days to come, a glimpse of the future? Or maybe even a warning that if I don't make the right decisions in my life then awful things will happen to me and others. Who knows? One thing is for certain anyway, I know for a fact I sure won't be able to forget about that dream for a long, long time to come.

As I walk down the street to collect my Belfast Telegraph newspapers for the day, I remind myself that I must remember to hide that big knife Minnis gave me at lunchtime today in a safe place where no-one will ever find it.

DAYS OF OUR LIVES

'Here is a box. A musical box. Wound up and ready to play.
But this box can hide a secret inside. Can you guess what is in
it today?' (Camberwick Green)

'I have lived in important places, times.' (Patrick Kavanagh,
Epic)

I am a time traveller. An explorer in other dimensions.

My mode of transport, however, is not a physical time
machine as such. I make my journeys lucidly through the
world of dreamscapes every night as I lay in my deep repose.
Sometimes I go sightseeing to the future, sometimes to the
past. But never existing in the present. Out of body, out of
universe experiences.

Occasionally I make expeditions to far reaching, exotic lands
that cannot be found on any human map or level of existence,
peopled by oddities which combine that of the real and the
unreal. Distant worlds popping up for a brief flame-like flicker
in a microscopic glimpse of awe-inspiring incongruous realms.
Before suddenly vanishing within themselves, retreating back
to the stuff of mystery, never to be reached again.

Last night, I made a wanderer's return - a pilgrimage
perhaps - to a defining memory from my past. One that is
forever etched in my mind, and although repressed for many
years since its happening, has always been there, lurking in the
background of my psyche, like a monster waiting to pounce
when the time is right. And the early hours of the morn was
the time it chose for its homecoming, in every defining vivid,

colourful detail.

This was the night in which I returned to 1987, from when I was a mere fledgling ten year old boy. An innocent, soon to be corrupted by the darkness of this world for the first time, bearing witness to a chain of events which would result in certain lives never being quite the same again...

***

'...The purple-headed mountains,
The river running by,
The sunset and the morning
That brightens up the sky.

All things bright and beautiful,
All creatures great and small,
All things wise and wonderful:
The Lord God made them all...'

We were at morning assembly once again, belting out the classics. Top tunes from the era, rockin' our socks. In many ways, these were glorious days. Times of playing conkers in the stony school yard, collecting frog spawn and blackberries in the surrounding fields, and catching the older lads sniffing glue. The generation of crazy mothers who could start a fight in an empty room (now they just do it on social media), checking the hairs on our heads for nits and fleas, and squinty, snot-covered smelly kids with verrucas. An era of teachers beating the shit out of us for the most minor of offences, Philly Hamill shitting in the leisure centre swimming pool for a lark, vomit-inducing school dinners served by angry old women, free EEC tinned meat all the rage, spitting on your crisps in the packet so nobody else would take any of them, lukewarm out-of-date school milk - the tops of which birds had just left their fresh droppings on, clunky BBC Micro computers, watching *Grange Hill* after teatime, being forced to play that awful-sounding, shrieking recorder instrument, listening to punk bands like the Sex Pistols and Peter and the Test Tube

Babies with my chum Reuben's older brother, and, of course, good old white dog shit. Oh, and that creepy old man who used to watch us from a distance when we had to do P.E. outside. A magical time of life - oh, to be young again!

Back then, I myself was a bit of an imaginative teller of dubious, not-quite-true tales. In essence, a spoofing little bastard. I once told my classmates and teacher that a man had tried to bungle/kidnap me into his red van on the Ligoniel Road, with malevolent intentions. The parents of the other pupils soon caught wind of it and were outraged, demanding immediate action. The police got involved too and after questioning me, determined it was all just one big fat whopping lie. Which, to be fair, it was.

But I wasn't the only liar in those days. One time, Ashleigh Ferguson relayed to me how there was a nun's head buried in the sandpit of the adjoining nursery. And Duffer once told me there was a monster - the fabled 'Ligoniel Beast' - roaming in the nearby hills. He said it was big and hairy, with huge claws and fangs, and ate children walking home from school alone. Even at the time I knew it was bollocks, and even if it was true, I couldn't help thinking that the creature would resemble something comical, like a cross between Bungle from *Rainbow* and Chewbacca from *Star Wars*.

Anyway, back to the assembly service. We finished our weak attempts at song, giggling once again at the '*purple headed mountains*' line, turning an innocent little chorus into some sort of smutty Sid James/*Carry On*-esque innuendo. Ooohhhh, matron! After all, in those days our sex education consisted mainly of finding tattered old dirty magazines in hedges and derelict houses, and, of course, some of those older boys enlightening us on the more gruesome details of the physical act of love, alongside fibs from them claiming to have slept with 'Page 3' girls. Yeah, right. Mr Weir, the bespectacled, chain-smoking and near-nervous wreck of a headmaster, stubbed out his cigarette in the blue-coloured tin ashtray at the side and took to the stage again. After a phlegm-filled cough, splutter and wheeze, he declared to his young audience that the *Lord's Prayer* would be recited next followed by the announcements, including a very special one indeed. This was to be a more exciting morning gathering than usual, it appeared. Whoopity-doo!

The first notices were more of the usual; it had been noted that money and some confectionery items had once more gone missing from the tuck shop. When the culprits were inevitably found, they would be suspended forthwith and their parents notified. Stealing was always wrong and a sin before the eyes of God, we were then advised gravely. The annual school magazine was looking submissions of drawings and stories. Children going on the school trip to Shannon in June needed to have the rest of their money in by Friday so to let our parents know, and practice for the school football team - the inappropriately titled (because we were crap), Ligoniel Lions - was to be held as usual after classes on Wednesday afternoon. The school nurse would also be on site soon to administer the rest of the BCG injections, although it was hoped there would not be an incident like the one from the previous year, when a kid had to be rushed to hospital after the nurse injected the wrong part of their arm.

And then to the big disclosure, as we waited with baited breath, to be introduced to a couple of real-life angels, as the other teachers in the front row - the Indian-born Mr Tandon (or Mr TanDOT as we kids would sometimes refer to him as, back when blatant racism was much more acceptable), the lanky, skeletal, long-fingered Miss McCullough and the stern Mrs Wilson - looked on fiercely with a bitter, jealous contempt.

These angels were actually a couple of brand new trainee teaching assistants, who would be spending the next couple of months in the pleasure of our company, sent to us by the university in Stranmillis via the local education and library board. Both in their early twenties, Miss Creswell was the golden-curled, blue-eyed, always smiling stunner, while her contemporary, Miss Neill, was the somewhat annoyingly fun-filled, voluptuous brunette, apparently high on simply life itself. For the vast majority of us children there that day, especially the boys, we fell in love instantly with these beautiful breaths of fresh air. A departure of great magnitude from the usual boring old faces we had become oh-so very used to over the years at our humbly populated place of learning.

But these charming, delightful young women had made a huge mistake in coming to our school on that fateful day, as twisted secrets concerning the habits of the staffroom at Ligoniel Primary School would soon be revealed, making headline news nationwide, and changing lives irrecoverably forever...

***

I was a P6 pupil in the springtime of 1987 when Miss Creswell and Miss Neill joined the ranks of our quaint little school's staff. Miss Creswell was assigned to my own class, which also consisted of the P5 pupils and whose commander in chief was Mr Tandon. Miss Neill helped look after the P7 kids under the beady eye of Mr Weir, the school principle who taught also. It was during one of my then regular Laurel and Hardy routines that Miss Creswell first attracted some negative attention by the main school staff.

Let me first of all indulge you by explaining what I mean exactly by 'Laurel and Hardy routine'. Every so often, for the amusement of himself and the other pupils, Mr Tandon would bring my friend, Fat Stevie the Liar, and myself up to front of the class and force us to do impressions of the legendary silent comedy duo. It seems that together, Fat Stevie and I resembled them greatly, myself of course playing Stan Laurel due to my gaunt, skinny countenance at the time. Mr Tandon would then get us to play out some of their sketches and catchphrases (*That's another fine mess you've gotten me into...* etc) whilst, along with the rest of our fellow pupils, laughing at us and pointing a mocking finger, exclaiming jovially in his very distinctive Indian accent, 'Look, look, everyone. It's Laurel and Hardy', whilst bursting into more fits of uncontrolled chortling. However, on this particular occasion, the well-meaning Miss Creswell, who was sitting at the back of the classroom looking on in a combination of shock and disbelief, was absolutely horrified at this public ridiculing of two children, despite how much fun everyone else was having, including Fat Stevie and I, who in reality always enjoyed the laughs and attention we got (well, I did anyway).

"Stop this at once, boys" she screamed patronisingly at us two performers at the front of the class, before continuing with, "Mr Tandon, may I have a word with you outside the classroom please? Right now!"

Mr Tandon ceased his laughing temporarily before letting all of us kids know that he'd only be a moment, his giggles returning as he walked past Oliver Hardy and I, halted mid-sketch, and outside the room to converse with an angered Miss Creswell in the corridor.

Us kids couldn't really make out properly what was being said between the two adults but it appeared Miss Creswell was upset and shouting something about it being "a complete disgrace" and how she was going to "report it all to the board". Mr Tandon was, it seemed, not taking her very seriously at all and telling her to "calm down" because it was all just "a bit of fun". After much discussion the two eventually re-entered the classroom where a now more visibly stern Mr Tandon ordered myself and my comedy partner to go back to our seats and that it was the end of the joviality and games for one day. This was just the first of one of many incidents in which the two new trainee teachers would rub the staff of Ligoniel Primary School up the wrong way.

Miss Neill took great offence at Mr Weir hitting one of his more unruly pupils, John Loftus, over the head with a metre rule. Collectively the two young women were unhappy at other discoveries they made, including the reveal of Mrs Wilson disciplining her pupils by smacking their bare bottoms with a wooden spoon, under performing, less able children being told straight to their faces that they were "thick", "retarded" and a "nincompoop" (whatever the fuck that is!) by most of the staff, the tuck shop being allowed to continue selling packets of crisps and other sweet stuff long past their 'sell by' dates to the kids, a blind eye being turned to pupils meeting up outside the school grounds with kids from the nearby rival St. Vincent De Paul school to engage in a spot of recreational rioting, and other happenings adjudged by the more politically correct twosome to be bang out of order.

The main body of four teachers, who had never taken to these meddling little upstarts from the very beginning, were getting a little bit pissed off to say the least. At their highly secretive meetings, which also included the caretaker, Mr McFarland, and the alcoholic Reverend Miskelly, who was involved in the school through the close-by St. Mark's Church, they discussed and plotted how they could save their jobs and livelihoods, not to mention the school itself, from this troublesome duo of mere girls straight out of university. But then the news broke to them that Miss Creswell and Miss Neill had indeed raised some contemptuous complaints with the education and library board and an investigation would be carried out in due course with the school, which was considered poorly attended and badly run anyway, now facing the very real possibility of definite closure for the first time since it originally opened its welcoming doors to the local community in 1964.

Word filtered out to the concerned parents that their little darlings might soon be without a place of education and they were not taking the news lightly. Almost straight away they took to the streets in protest. Well, outside the school gates anyway. Big Maggie 'Swing the Bacon' was the ringleader, threatening to 'knock the fuck out of' anyone who disagreed with her and shouting stuff about how 'no bastardin fucker was ever going to rob her kids of an eduction'. Her second-in-command and main creator of the protest signs was the big-titted Maureen, whom it looked like always had two large basketballs stuffed up her jumper. The angry parents' placards displayed bold statements on colourfully-inked pieces of card, slogans such as, 'SOS - SAVE OUR SCHOOL!', 'FIGHT THE CLOSURE!' and 'EDUCATION IS A RIGHT OUR CHILDREN WILL NOT BE DENIED!'.

It was around the time of these protests that some sinister and well dressed men and women began showing up at the school randomly. These odd characters never smiled or engaged in conversation with us kids or even the teachers themselves, including the now very much detested by the other staff, Miss Creswell and Miss Neill. At first, everyone seemed to just automatically assume they were inspectors from the eduction and library board, but as they continued to pop up more frequently, often seated at the back of the classrooms, closely monitoring all around them and keeping a close eye especially on the two student trainee teachers, us kids began having other ideas as to who these mysterious, silent people who dressed like Mormons really were. It was the generally held belief that they were in a position of great power in one way or the other. They were either here to look over and report on our main body of teachers, or Miss Creswell and Miss Neill, or both. Any attempt at striking up a conversation with them was usually met with a muted shake of the head. After almost a couple of weeks of their irregular appearances, they suddenly ceased being there altogether. Their sudden showing up and even more sudden disappearance was never properly explained to any of us pupils or our parents, either back then or in the years following. They would simply just show up every now and again over a couple of weeks, intensely watch everything that was going on, before eventually ceasing to exist in the school ever again.

Things seemed to be returning to a normality of sorts at the school for a few weeks, although there was still the constant tension between the teachers and the trainees and, of course, the rumours of closure still hung heavy in the air, although not quite as strongly. A couple of days before we quit for our long-awaited eight week summer break, some of us youngsters made a discovery so grisly it has been scarred deep into our minds in such a strong fashion that we have still never been able to properly forget about it, it remaining freshly clear in some dark corner of our heads right up until this very day in 2018, decades later.

It was a sunny Thursday afternoon as my best friends and I made our usual walk to school. Suzanne Vega's *Luka* was blasting from a car radio somewhere. Everyone was in cheerful form, including the birds in the sky who were chirping a happy song. As per usual, before assembly in the gym, my mates, Jonny McCoubrey and Sparky, and I hung around the playground kicking football and chatting idly about the upcoming summer holidays. We decided upon heading up to the assembly hall a couple of minutes early, as we often did, so that we could get good seats at the back beside each other. On that particular morning, we were actually the first ones to walk up the back stairs of the school towards the gym which doubled as an assembly and concert hall. For some reason, the long, dusty dark purple curtains were pulled across the windowed doors from the inside. Perhaps the caretaker, Mr McFarland, was off sick and so no-one had opened up the assembly hall yet? My friend, Jonny, tried the door handle anyway. It was unlocked. He opened it up and the three of us unsuspectingly peeled back the heavy purple drapes, to be greeted with a crime scene of unimaginable horror, one unfit for the eyes of any stable adult, never mind those of the mere children we were.

None of the assembly seats had been put in place in the hall and they were all stacked neatly at the right hand side of the room. The wooden floor of our gym/assembly hall was awash with a dark red liquid. The blood was everywhere - splattered over the walls, the front of the curtains and even on the ceiling. Written on the walls, daubed in said blood, were strange words and symbols, unidentifiable to us kids then, though possibly Latin or some other ancient Biblical language. It was my young friend Sparky who drew our attention to the back left hand wall where the climbing bars were situated for use in P.E. class. Hanging upside down on the climbing bars was a body. That of a female, it appeared. Her head had been removed completely, blood still dripping from the crude gash on her neck where it had been severed, crucified like the apostle Peter, but for very different reasons apparently. Jonny, Sparky and I stood frozen in a profound state of shock as some of the other kids started piling into the assembly hall, discovering the morbid horror show all for themselves.

In the screaming, chaos and insanity which was to follow, some of the other children ran instinctively to their classrooms. My younger five year old sister, Catherine, was one of those kids to do just that and when she and her little friend, Sarah, burst through their classroom door in a terror they couldn't even fully comprehend at such a youthful age they were welcomed with the decapitated head - eyes still frozen wide open in abject terror - of the once bubbly Miss Neill on top of Mrs Wilson's classroom piano. It was a summer morning none of us would ever forget for the rest of our lives.

In the following days and weeks a full police investigation ensued and many, many questions were asked. Despite making news headlines right across Great Britain and beyond and most local people believing the teachers were involved in some way or had even arranged it, the staff of Ligoniel Primary School were cleared of all wrongdoing and the school was eventually allowed to reopen for good a few months later with a brand new staff of freshly-faced new teachers, who actually looked a lot like children's television presenters, now in place, replacing the tired and weary (and suspected of a double murder!) ones. Our old teachers were sent to work in different schools around the country. The head of Miss Creswell, who was officially identified as the crucified body in the gym, and body of Miss Neill, the owner of the head placed neatly on the classroom piano, were never found.

The strong widely held belief that our original teaching staff of Mr Weir, Mr Tandon, Miss McCullough and Mrs Wilson were involved in some sort of Satanic cult back then is still unproven but populates the pages of many books written in the aftermath and quite a few modern 'real life horror' websites to this day.

As for us children, we got over it all rather quickly. Kids are pretty resilient like that. We did receive some quite pointless counselling over the years, but in general terms, despite never being able to forget it, it didn't really affect us that much psychologically, although our memories of the more nightmarish details did become suppressed somewhat. It could even be argued that we were made of much sterner stuff back then, learning to grow up the hard way in many cases.

Regardless, the moral of this story - if there even is one - is not to mess with the old guard, especially if they are embroiled in a nefarious Satanic cult hell-bent on bloody vengeance.

(**STORY NOTES**: This tale is dedicated to the real Ligoniel Primary School. They truly were the days of our lives.)

AN ANAGRAM OF FUNERAL IS REAL FUN

All those women crying and all those sugar-laden cups of tea. Sandwiches too. Cut into neat little triangles. They had egg 'n onion. They had cheese and tomato. They had tuna. They even had some of that lovely ham from Jackie's butchers on the Shankill Road. Something for everyone. And sarnies made with real butter too, not that processed 'low in fat, polyunsaturated' margarine crap that you get nowadays in your local corporate Tesco or Asda store. What the fuck does 'polyunsaturated' mean anyway? No, we had the real deal back then. Such a shame I got a rather substantial hair in my otherwise very tasty egg 'n onion bap, however. Fuckin' old people, with their unwelcome hairs and unusual obsession with tea, biscuits and sandwiches. Probably a moustache hair from one of the old women too. Or maybe even a stray from one of their purple rinses. I mean, who on God's earth dyes their hair purple? I get that they are trying to hide the great shame of unwanted greys, but why not a nice bottle blonde or brunette instead? Purple just makes them look like an extra from *A Clockwork Orange*. I guess when you reach a certain age of decrepitude, your dietary and hairstyling tastes must take a sudden nosedive for the worse. Ah, well, I suppose I should be grateful that it wasn't a pubic hair. At least not that I know of, anyway.

It was 1984. I was seven years old and attending the funeral of my great-granny at her old terraced house in Ainsworth Street in the Woodvale area. It was my first proper experience of death and the first time I ever saw a dead body. A rather exciting and unforgettable experience it was too.

The woman with whom everyone had congregated to remember at this particular wake, was a very good and decent woman of Quaker stock. Hard-working all her long life, in the old linen mills of Belfast, and the raising of five daughters and three sons, Mrs Carson had not had an easy life of it, really due to the terrible poverty and social deprivation of the working classes of the time, and also because of her alcoholic, brutish husband, who himself had died prematurely after accidentally drinking a glass of bleach. Although to be fair, and with hindsight, he was probably suffering from a form of post traumatic stress after witnessing the full horrors of the Great War, including the Battle of the Somme, first hand from the front line. His good wife, and reason for us gathering on this day, was a tall and slender lady, tough as old boots, but in the nicest possible way. She had to be like that, to survive life. Women of her ilk are the real heroes of this world.

My great-granny was in a better place now, or so young me was told that day - the very same thing I was told at other future funerals as well. A place with no more pain or suffering. A blissfully tranquil place where the lion lies down with the lamb. And so forth. That's right, my ninety-year-old great-grandmother was now in Heaven. Apparently. She certainly deserved to be in a place like that, but if you ask me, Heaven - with all its tedious boredom and being packed-to-the rafters with those old relatives that you never actually liked in the first place - sounds a lot more like Hell. Fuck that shit! But I'm digressing now, so I'll get back to the funeral.

Those black-suited men were knocking back the beers and holding it together quite impressively, with a steely resolve and stiff upper lip. How very of the time. They were gathered around the stern oak coffin which contained the remains of the also stern, but kind, old woman, her final place of rest in this world. Her three sons - Frank (the greying, sensible big brother-type), Robert (the hard-working shipyard worker with slicked back, jet black hair) and David (the weirdly quiet, red-haired one) - were bidding their last farewells and wishes of love and thanksgiving for her long and generous life. A single solitary tear was running down the left cheek of my uncle David.

I remember it was raining heavily on that miserable overcast October day. Autumn, with its falling leaves and decreasing temperatures, was at its peak. The rather large coffin, surrounded by bouquets of wild and colourful flowers, appeared even more hugely domineering at the front window of the tiny terraced homestead. That, and the fact I was obviously much smaller back then, made the whole world appear quite titanic to me.

The mainly adult crowd was packed into the humble home, regaling each other with tales of the hard old days and paying tribute to the woman at the very centre of things. I recall the strangely-patterned, blue and purple, art-deco-esque 1970s wallpaper, part of it peeling off at the corners of the front window due to damp setting in. A portable black and white telly with an aerial was in the right-hand corner of the front of the living room (these were, of course, more simpler times of just three channels available, long before the advent of multi-media platforms and thon interweb-thingy), with a basic wooden coffee table on top of a bright green rug in the centre, beside the sofa. There was a glass ashtray filled with cigarette butts on top of it. The old working scullery remains vivid in my mind also, its orangey-yellow lino flooring and wallpaper etched firmly into my memory banks. And how could I forget that chillingly cold and uncomfortable outdoor toilet, along with its hard and roughly cemented floor, and hard-to-reach (for a young boy) flushing chain? I you ask me, outdoor toilets are much more hygienic than the modern, fancy indoor ones. I mean, who really wants to take a shit in the same general area where one has to eat, sleep and live? Bring back the outdoor bogs, I say!

It was as the three sons of Mrs Carson moved away from the coffin and lit up their hand-rolled cigarettes, that things really began to take a turn towards the rather unusual, in a most unexpected, unforgettable turn of events.

One of the few children there that day (aside from myself), was my four year old cousin - the pig-tailed, ginger-haired and freckle-faced Lucy - who was standing on a chair morbidly inspecting the old dear's body with a great fascination. She soon ceased with her fixation and looked up and exclaimed, with a certain twisted elation, that she had just seen the dearly departed's eyes blink.

"Nonsense, you silly girl!" was the general consensus of the adults.

"But, she did, she did! I'm telling you. Look, she's doing it again!" screamed the annoying little brat with the lisp, in her tiny red dress, black buckle-up shoes, and white socks up to her knees.

Some of the adults moved over to the open coffin to inspect and what was to follow will always be remembered by those of us there to witness such an astonishing, curious happening, a happening that was never spoken of again - swept under the carpet with the rest of the sordidly dark family secrets, due to the highly controversial and damning nature of it all.

To the massive shock of all and sundry in the room, Mrs Sarah Barbara Carson's eyes were indeed flickering, just before she jumped up straight in her coffin with a tight jolt, suddenly opening her peepers wide, lifting up her right arm, and pointing her withering, wrinkled index finger at my uncle David, whilst shrieking at the top of her voice in a deafening, shrill high-pitched tone:

"IT WAS HIM, IT WAS HIM! HE DID THIS TO ME! THIS IS ALL MY EVIL SON DAVID'S FAULT!"

With that, her mouth let out a final gasp, the dark eyes on her face rolling back into its skeletal head, the elderly lady falling back inside the coffin, never to awaken again from her ancient slumber.

In the direct aftermath, my aunt Evelyn fainted and had to be rushed to hospital by ambulance, whilst the rest of the mourners were numbed in a state of continued disarray - some screaming, some weeping furiously, some even arguing with each other, with many questions and accusations being thrown around, especially at my now very much defensive uncle David, who initially denied any knowledge of what his not-quite-dead mother had unbelievably just done.

The funeral itself went ahead eventually, later than originally planned, after a local doctor was called to make sure the old woman was really dead and everyone else had somewhat calmed down a bit. In the weeks that were to follow, uncle David Carson confessed to his sister, my aunt Evelyn, that he had poisoned and smothered his own mother in her sleep, to gain her measly financial inheritance that he was desperate for after his printing business had collapsed, leaving him in debt and ruin. A family cover up ensued, due to fear of the massive embarrassment and shame the scandal would no doubt bring upon the good family name. It appears that keeping up appearances and public images was more important than the truth and life of an innocent kindly old lady, to my family.

I never forgot it, however, and never will. In the resulting years, every single time I attended another funeral as an adult, I would always recall to myself - with more than a little edge of ghoulish glee - the strange events of that macabre day from my childhood.

(**STORY NOTES**: This is a highly fictionalised version of some of my very earliest memories attending the funeral of my great-grandmother in 1981, aged four. The story is therefore dedicated to her memory, Mrs Sarah Speers.)

A CACOPHONY OF VOICES

The young woman sat alone on an old wooden chair in the filthy room, the mysterious envelope placed neatly on her lap. She lit up a cigarette and eye-balled her surroundings.

The house was an old terraced one in the Shankill area of West Belfast. Technically she owned the house, as Peter, her estate agent husband had acquired it some weeks prior with the intention of renovating it before renting it out. She had pinched the keys from her other half's office earlier that morning when she called in to see him on the pretence that she just felt like rewarding her hard working sweetheart with a well deserved sandwich. A chicken and mayo sandwich it was too, his favourite.

The interior of the Battenberg Street home was in some serious ruin. The 1970s-style brown and yellow patterned wallpaper was ripped throughout, stained and adorned with graffiti, while at some point the living room ceiling had caved in. Some Robin Hood-style cheeky chappies, presumably local men, had apparently cleared the empty house of anything of value, including the copper wiring, radiators and carpets, the previous elderly owners long since gone, the wife having passed away and the widower husband now residing in a nearby care home. The debris of empty bottles and cans of alcohol, along with joint roaches appeared to be the work of local youths looking somewhere to crash.

The woman was very apprehensive about opening the envelope. She could have opened it at home but she didn't want to expose her two young daughters to whatever essence its inside may have been holding. If what she was told was true then its contents could quite possibly bring a great curse upon her, but she was profoundly intrigued by it also, maybe even obsessed. Since she was a small girl she had always had a great interest in all things occult-related, the mysterious. As a teenager, she regularly played on a Ouija board with her best friend, Laura. They did everything together after becoming close friends when they first met in P1, their very first year of primary school. They sat beside each other in school for twelve years, liked the same pop stars and shared their deepest secrets on boys together. *Here comes trouble now* and *the terrible twins* are just a couple of the things people would say whenever they saw them together. Their October birthdays were only a week apart and their first jobs were the same as well, together in the HCL call centre in town. Tragedy struck when they were twenty-one, however, after Laura collapsed during a rave at a nightclub named Xanadu situated somewhere in the countryside. Laura had been taking illegal substances on her best friend's behest, never regaining consciousness, officially pronounced dead a few hours later at a nearby hospital. The Ouija board itself had been given to the woman as a child by her maternal grandmother, who oft claimed to be a witch who could make contact with none other than the deceased themselves, but the silly old dear was never taken quite seriously by anyone at all.

It was a grey, overcast day outside, looking like it was about to pour with rain at any moment. From the small front window the woman could see and hear some boys in the street playing football, joking and laughing with each other. *They better not hit my bloody car with that ball!* she thought to herself, overprotective as always of the flashy, expensive sports car her rich husband had presented her with a year prior as a random gift for the love of his life. She looked at the envelope situated on top of her tartan skirt. Her name and the address she was currently at was inked in the most beautiful handwriting, quite possibly even calligraphy. The person in America whom she had contacted via the dark web, and went by the user name *Mephistopheles76*, obviously had some talent.

After nervously playing with her long red locks for a while, the woman decided she was being silly and it was time to open up the contents of the letter. She reckoned she was being daft for even being interested in the dark arts at all, as many had told her over the years, including Peter. *A load of old horse shit, the biggest lot of mumbo-jumbo ever, nonsense old wives' tales* he would tell her with a scorning mockery. She couldn't help it though. The real world was boring and tedious at the best of times. It was just a bit of harmless fun, a little bit of intrigue and an interest she had obviously inherited from her mother and her mother before her.

Suddenly, she lifted up the letter in both hands and violently ripped off the white paper envelope revealing its contents to her. It was an old black and white photograph.

The picture had been weathered over the years and looked faded somewhat with a crease at the top right hand corner. It featured some some small black children, boys and girls, all pre-teens apparently aged around ten years or less. They were standing together in a meadow of sorts, facing the camera with their arms linked. None of them were smiling, all looking rather gravely towards the camera. The girl in the centre was wearing an extremely unsettling, malevolent-looking demonic mask. Below the picture, written on its edge, was the following: *The Children of Chax, Republic of Haiti, 1932.*

The woman studied the picture for around a minute. *This is indeed all so very silly*, she ruminated. *Peter will make fun of me if he finds out and he will be just right to, especially when he notices that his bank account is a little lighter this month after I paid five hundred pounds of his hard earned cash to obtain this apparently very rare and cursed image. It's all pretty ridiculous like he says, sitting alone in an empty house on the Shankill and staring at an old photo. Probably another foolish victim of an internet scam.*

She stared in silence at the photograph for another couple of minutes before deciding it was time to leave and get back into her car, putting all this nonsense behind her and making the drive back to County Down. She reckoned she could maybe hit the gym for an hour or two, to help release all this nervous tension inside her.

As she stood up and went to slip the photo into her blouse pocket, she jumped back after noticing, or at very least thinking she noticed, something out of the corner of her eye. She could have sworn the image on the picture moved a little.

She quickly put the photo up to the front of her face and studied it in detail, her eyes narrowing as she focused in on it. What she saw made her heart sink, causing her to grab out for the wooden chair, fumbling a little for it and then sitting back down again on it, not once blinking or taking her eyes off the image. She reckoned it was probably just her imagination, or some sort of optical illusion, a trick of the light, but she was almost certain the little girl in the demonic mask had moved forward a few steps. *Yes, she definitely did! All those kids were in a straight line before, but now she has moved forward a little! This is really weird.* The woman blinked.

Intensely, she zoned in on the photograph for quite a few minutes, noting every single detail. Focusing in, focusing in, focusing in. And then it happened. The children in the photograph began to move. Slightly at first, but then casually in front of the woman's very eyes, in almost three dimensions, all the children, in their torn, ragged clothing, moving forward a few strides and then forming a circle, arms linked once again. The circle of young Caribbean kids then moved anti-clockwise in the circle, before the masked girl broke from the chain and into the centre. There she danced a strange dance, contorting her body in impossible ways, whilst the other youngsters chanted an incantation, some sort of dark prayer perhaps, something unholy presumably, in a rhythmic, repetitive unnatural tone.

The woman dropped the photograph onto the floor in a panicked haste and buried her face in her hands, rubbing her eyes, both horrified and astonished at the same time. When she eventually removed her hands and opened her eyes again she stared down at the picture on the ground. It was just as it was when she first witnessed it. Not moving. Back to normal. Still and silent.

What the fuck is going on here? This can't be real. This must be some sort of magic trick or prank. Or maybe I'm having an acid flashback or the like from my days as a raver. No way can this be real!

She stared at the photograph and then into space for quite some time.

Then a window inside her mind opened up and strange voices began talking incessantly inside her head.

Timid, quiet, slow at first:

Hello, can you hear me?

Where are you?

Where am I?

I can't see.

It's dark down here, so very dark.

Are you here? I've been having bad dreams again, my dear.

Most of the voices were female, desperate sounding. Some of them were male, but they were mostly unintelligible and very difficult to understand. The female voices were familiar, but becoming distant, before suddenly increasing in tone and volume again:

We are in the dark place now, the neverending region of everlasting pain.

Humiliation all around us.

Save us, please!

We are the damned ones.

Can you hear us?

Swiftly, there were loud screams from the voices before returning to the chattering again, but this time in sentences of gibberish, nonsensical words, almost as if they were speaking backwards. Then the voices turned extremely nasty, cursing and verbally abusing the woman with taunts of a sexual nature - *Whore! Cocksucker! Bastard slut-child Jezebel!*

The woman could now hear her grandmother's voice in there cursing her too. The voices and background screams increased in noise level again, speaking faster and faster, louder and louder, reaching an unbearable level. The woman stood up quickly and put her hands on her head, shaking it violently whilst crying and screaming and begging the voices to stop, but they refused to relent, becoming more and more intensified. Then a very well-known voice spoke loudly over the rest of the tormenting cries. It was that of her dead best friend, Laura, and she was screeching:

You fucking bitch. I hate you! You bought those drugs on that night I died. The ones that fucking killed me! I didn't want to take them, but you made me. You put the pressure on me. You promised me it would be fun. You swore that no harm would come to us. But it did - well, to me anyway. I **hate** *you. You fucking murdered me!*

The woman screamed out, "I'm sorry, Laura! I'm so, so sorry!"

The other voices reached a fever pitch, screaming and cursing and insulting and bellowing inside of the woman's head, more and more, angrier and angrier, until some sort of switch inside her mind flicked and she lost her sanity completely, dropping to the floor beside the old black and white photograph, soon slipping out of consciousness. The last thing she saw before fading away into darkness was the photo beside her, a new image now engrained on it, at the front of the line of young Haitian children. It was a face. A face not of this world, one of pure maliciousness, of depravity and Satanic intent. The face was a combination of the woman's own face and that of the mask the little girl in the picture was wearing. An image that in itself could send even the very strongest of minds into the depths of despair with a profound fear.

***

Peter drove straight to the mental health facility as soon as the police had contacted him about the incident with his wife in the derelict house on the Shankill. They had been alerted by one of the mothers of some local boys who had heard screaming and broke into the house to find the woman face down on the floor, collapsed and out cold. They tracked Peter down through the personalised number plate on the fancy sports car in front of the house she had arrived in.

The doctor at the hospital allowed Peter to visit his wife in the room where she was being monitored and kept for her own safety. She was conscious but unresponsive, her face frozen in a look of abject terror, eyes wide open and unblinking.

When the woman's desperately concerned husband enquired as to what had happened to her he was met with shrugs and shakes of the head. Although examinations on her were apparently ongoing, her preliminary diagnosis was that she had fallen victim to some extreme, sudden shock.

As Peter went to leave the hospital and alert relatives of the situation, he was called back by one of the male psychiatric nurses who had forgotten to give him his wife's possessions, found on her at the time she was discovered: a packet of cigarettes, a lighter, a set of keys, an iPhone and an old crumpled photograph. Peter put the belongings into his pocket and glanced at the photo of the small black children in the meadow. He thought it odd that his wife would have such an item in her possession and couldn't quite understand it at all.

After placing the photo into the inside pocket of the jacket of his designer suit, he got into his car and decided he would head straight home and study this strange picture some more.

THE DEVIL CAME AND TOOK ME

'Hey diddle diddle,
The cat and the fiddle,
The cow jumped over the moon.
The little dog laughed,
To see such fun,
And the dish ran away with the spoon.'
(Old nursery rhyme)

Late January, 2008

Being sober is being forced to conform to society's imposed norms. One becomes enslaved to an unemotional and unattractive machine, mere cogs in a system of creative and intellectual oppression that does not love us back. This is of particular relevance to the working classes. The only real releases from this waking nightmare are to get regularly and intentionally out of one's proverbial tree on mood-altering substances and, of course, death itself, but as Irvine Welsh once so sagely stated, death will probably be shite too. Going on a massive fuck off hedonistic bender for a few days and nights, involving alcohol and illegal drugs, is a massive two-fingered salute at this selfish integral organisation of orderliness, and it feels pretty damn good too, in many ways. In short, fuck the system.

These were just some of the racing thoughts slipping through Stevie Brown's mind that day, as he left his place of employment on a half day leave pass. Stevie hated his job at the call centre. He particularly detested those stupid, ignorant, whiny, rude, dumb fuck members of the public who called in to him every day, with their incessant idiotic questions and complaints of a highly tedious and easily-resolved nature. The general public were major league assholes, in fact he pretty much loathed the vast majority of the human race, save for one or two rare exceptions. As Stevie headed to the nearest bar he could find, more thoughts filled his head.

Life is not a film, nor a book of fiction. It is very real and any bad decisions you make will have serious repercussions which can sometimes take many years to become realised. You reap what you sow. A happy ending is never guaranteed. In fact, when you really think about it, since all of our lives will end in death and whatever idea of Heaven or Hell each individual has in their mind is definitely not a certainty, then technically every life has an unhappy ending. That said, there can be good, even great, times in between but you really are the author of your own destiny so try your very hardest not to fuck it up, despite what fate has bestowed upon you. Being an alcoholic and/or addict is far from a glamorous existence, despite what many idiotic wankers will have you believe. Addiction to mood-altering substances, whatever your drug of choice may be, will degrade you in the extreme - you will do things that in sobriety would both shock and disgust you. But this not being enough, you will continually return to the scene of the crime for more of the same on a seemingly continuous, neverending loop until there is a break in the cycle, through either an epiphany of clarity or the aforementioned death. Now, that is insanity, or at very least some form of personality disorder.

There is, of course, always a choice every time the addict/alcoholic is faced with this dilemma in the form of cravings or otherwise, despite how greyed and muddied the waters can very often appear. Two year old children diagnosed with leukemia or born with HIV don't have a choice, but the addict will often happily ignore his own choice and continue to wallow in his selfish desires and self pity. His or her self-destructive nature is something of a pleasure to behold to them, however, in that whatever madness and pain lies in front of them is well deserving in their minds. And the temporary numbing of their pain is well worth it for a short period of euphoria, One thing they are promised in addition, however, is many future years - if they survive long enough, that is - filled with unhappiness, depression and regret, looking back over a life of 'what could have beens'. Every single choice we make in this life will therefore define the quality - or lack of it - of our remaining time on this dying planet, climaxing with that previously referenced unhappy ending. So choose wisely.

Despite knowing much better than what most others in his shoes do, Stevie entered the first bar he got to anyway. He'd also decided somewhere along the line that he had just quit his job for good this time.

Hunter's bar on the Lisburn Road area of South Belfast was the nearest to the call centre and it would do just rightly. It wasn't a bad joint really. Just like the area where it was based it could probably be best described as working class trying to be middle class. Quite the multi-cultural area of the city too, it is also home to quite a large student populace, many of them being educated at the close by Queen's University. It's a pretty nice area actually and the perfect place for an alcoholic to frequent for a nice quiet pint or twenty, away from the hustle and bustle of the main city centre and certain 'local' bars on all sides of the political persuasion, full to the brim with paramilitaries and wankers. Stevie even had his own name for the district - 'Studentville' - and he certainly didn't have a problem drinking anywhere that sold his particular brand of poison and over the years had drank in almost literally every part of the town (a spot of cross community partying never bothered him at all) and further afield. But these days, when he did decide to go on a bender, he just wanted somewhere quiet with a jukebox and where nobody knew him. The fact that his workplace was located in such an area was even more convenient, for good and for bad.

The first couple of pints were bliss and were downed rather quickly indeed (as per usual). Stevie could relax properly now, his mind becoming more at ease, enjoying himself more as his inhibitions slowly but surely slithered away. Until the inevitable nightmare gradually began, of course, one that is always in the post the moment the first drink is taken.

As the youngish man (Stevie was now in his early thirties) got up to put on a few tunes from the jukebox he noticed a handsome man with dark hair, eyes and features - on first appearance in his early fifties - watching him select his songs from the machine with flashing lights. Stevie didn't really pay much attention to him though. He was more concerned about his musical choices. He was in the mood for a bit of Oasis, to remind him of his more youthful days of the 1990s.

As Noel Gallagher crooned about making Sally wait and not to look back in anger, Stevie's mind relaxed even more, the chemicals from the alcohol already in his system helping him on his voyage through the temporarily extremely contented stage of the binge, now at true peace with the universe, everything at last making sense - worries, trials and tribulations now long gone. The key word here being temporary, the heightened state of nirvana never lasting.

Another couple of pints of Harp lager later, Stevie decided it was almost time to go on the cider. To him, there was nothing quite like a delicious pint glass of fermented apples with ice. A acquired taste, yes, but for the cider connoisseur like him these moments were to be cherished.

Jarvis Cocker was now emanating from the music system, performing Pulp's *Razzmatazz*, as Stevie sat down with his sweet-tasting glass of apple-based beverage. He thought to himself how underrated a band Pulp were back in the mid-90s. His tipsy notions then reverted back to his childhood days of stage magic. As a pre-teen he was a keen amateur magician, learning the tricks of the trade through books and magic sets, often given to him as Christmas or birthday presents. He was a regular customer of his local town centre joke shops too. When he and his family used to holiday at his uncle's caravan in County Down, Stevie used to perform magic shows for them at night, dazzling all and sundry with his mysterious, inexplicable card tricks and sleight of hand. He now regretted not continuing with this hobby into adulthood. Who knows where it may have taken him? Perhaps performing shows all over the world, like David Blaine or Paul Daniels, the latter whom he used to watch as a kid. He would probably now even have become an esteemed member of the illustrious 'Magic Circle'. But when those awkward teenage years came, his love of the shocking and entertaining of audiences soon faded. There was also that little incident in the Isle of Man when he was thirteen and away on his holidays once more with his parents and sisters.

At the time he considered himself too old to be doing things with his mum, dad and two younger sisters, so he wandered around Douglas on his own for a lot of the holiday and one night wound up at a hypnotist's show in some old theatre building. When the hypnotist was looking for volunteers from the audience to be brought on stage and put in a trance, Stevie excitedly put up his hand and was selected alongside a few other willing punters game for a laugh. Alas, it soon to be discovered first hand by the young lad that the hypnotist was indeed a fraud and this disappointment had a profound effect on him, in part fuelling his deep cynicism with the world in his adult years. Expecting to be properly put into a trance and mentally controlled by the showman, Stevie was never really hypnotised at all by the man and simply played along with his commands for two reasons - to placate the intimidating hypnotist and also because he was on stage in front of a considerable audience, so felt the necessity to perform, in this particular case pretending he could see a monkey chasing him around the stage. Monkey business indeed. The next day, when he bumped into a bunch of older guys in their twenties from Dublin, who recognised him from his stage antics and whose friend was also one of the audience members brought to the stage, they relayed to him that their friend also wasn't really hypnotised either, confirming Stevie's suspicions that the hypnotist was indeed one big fat liar and fake.

Stevie went outside in the cold winter's afternoon for a smoke, the new ban on smoking in public places now well in place. It was just beginning to snow as some goth youths passed him at the front of the bar and after some conversing amongst each other finally decided to go into Hunter's for a drink also. Stevie reckoned if he ever did get back into the stage magic he would hire a goth girl as his glamorous assistant. Goth girls were so fucking sexy to him, with their colourful hairstyles, extreme piercings, strange tattoos and slutty revealing outfits. Once he finished his cigarette he tossed it onto the pavement, stood on it and went back inside to go for a piss before returning to his drink.

As he stood at the urinal relieving himself, Stevie couldn't help but feel that he was being watched by a man who had followed him into the toilet and was now standing beside the sink. It was the darkly featured chap whom he had noticed earlier sitting on the other side of the bar, drinking presumably whiskey or some sort of other spirit in a small glass. After finishing his piss and buttoning up his jeans, Stevie turned around to find that this weird man was indeed staring at him intently, watching his every move. Stevie decided upon an attempt at breaking the awkwardness.

"Hello there. How's it going?"

No reply. Just more intense staring.

"Are you okay, mate? What's the crack here, have you got some sort of problem or what?"

The man eventually spoke in an odd, dreary tone.

"Sorry. My apologies. I've just been watching you for a bit, that's all. No harm intended. You caught my attention when you first came into the bar and I've been watching you ever since. Sorry, where are my manners? Pleased to meet you. My name is Augustus."

Augustus held out his hand for Stevie to shake. Stevie nervously, gently shook it back.

"Good to meet you too, Augustus, but what were you staring at me for? What's that all about then? Look, if this is what I think it is then I have to say I'm flattered but I'm just not that way inclined. Anyway, look after yourself. I'm away for another liquor here."

As Stevie exited the small, confined toilet with his back to Augustus, the man chased after him, halting him by placing his hand tightly on his right shoulder, forcing Stevie to spin around.

"Look, look, let me buy you a drink. I promise you it's not what you think, not at all. I think I might know you from somewhere, that's all. That's why I was staring at you. Sorry if I freaked you out a bit. I mean you no harm. Please, let me buy you a drink to apologise."

"Listen, mate. Don't worry about it, honestly. No biggie, no harm done. Don't worry about the drink either."

Stevie actually wanted to accept the offer of the drink, as he didn't have that much money on him and for his binge to continue as he planned he was going to have to phone someone to borrow some cash pretty soon. He was simply faking politeness until the guy inevitably asked him again.

"Look, I don't mind, I really don't. And I honestly think I do know you from somewhere. Look, I'm having a Jack Daniels on the rocks. Do you want one too?"

"Okay then, you've twisted my arm. Make mine a Jack and white lemonade though. I'll be sitting over in the corner there."

"Coming right up. Oh, by the way, what's you're name?"

"Stevie."

"Good to meet you, Stevie. I'll just be two shakes of a lamb's tail."

As Augustus went to the bar to order the drinks, Stevie went back to his seat wondering if this was such a good idea after all. Maybe he should just have the one drink with the man then split. He just wanted to be alone and get out of his tree anyway. Perhaps he should head for home, get a lend of some more money from somewhere and purchase a massive carry out which would do him well into tomorrow. Augustus soon returned with the drinks and they got chatting again.

The two men talked for more than an hour over a few rounds of drinks, tedious small talk at first, followed eventually by a conversation of more substance. They both spoke of their shared hatred of their jobs. Augustus explained that he was an English professor at Queen's University and how the job was beginning to drain him, physically and mentally. He had nothing but contempt for his bureaucratic superiors (only interested in statistics and money) and the current batch of students currently studying at the well respected place of learning. Stevie spoke to the strange Augustus about how he had just walked out of his job at the call centre, having had simply enough of stupid fuckers hurling abuse at him over the phone line and his whiny little manager, Scott Large.

"I don't blame you, Stevie. I couldn't stick it in one of those places either. All that abuse and nonsense you have to put up with. No way."

"Yea, and for really shitty pay too."

"Minimum wage?"

"Not a kick in the arse off it."

"No, it wouldn't be my scene. At least you don't have to put up with a bunch of spoilt millennials with a self-entitlement complex. So what are you going to do with yourself now?"

"What's a millennial when it's at home?"

"The youth of today. Kids born after 1985 or the like. Generation Y. I believe it has something to do with a bunch of murders which happened to some kids in America back then. Ever since that event children in general there were mollycoddled and overprotected much, much more. They were told that whenever they grew up they could be literally whatever they wanted and go into any field of work they wished, which, as you know, is nonsense. They were only told positive stuff about themselves, the 'everyone gets a medal' sort of attitude, where they were never properly shown how to deal with failure in life in their formative years, resulting in a new generation of adults who genuinely believe they are entitled to everything they want. Without the laborious hard work, time and effort, of course. As per usual, these attitudes transferred across the Atlantic. It's not actually the fault of the kids that they such are a bunch of self-obsessed brats. The problem lies with their parents and society as whole. The emergence of the internet, instant messaging and so on has made things even worse, as they now not only demand everything they want, but demand it all straight away. So anyway, enough of my incessant ramblings, what are your plans now that you have quit your job?"

"Ah, I get you now. Thank fuck I grew up as a member of Generation X then. I dunno. I'll be on the piss for a few days now, borrowing and begging no doubt. But once I recover from this I'll eventually sort myself out and find a new job. Not another fuckin' call centre though."

"A few days of drinking? That's quite a lot. What about your poor liver?"

"Fuck my liver. It's hasn't caused me any problems yet. And

anyway, I can't help it."

"You seem quite drunk now and you're fairly putting those drinks away. Are you an alcoholic?"

"Pretty much. For all intents and purposes. An illness of mind, body and soul I've been told."

"Do you go to AA?"

"Tried it. That and rehab. I wouldn't knock them, as they have helped so many - countless numbers really - over the years, but let's just say they never really worked for me. I learnt some really good stuff from them, stuff about myself but I suppose, at the end of the day, it really has to come from deep within myself. Maybe I just don't want to give up drinking right now. I dunno."

"I understand."

"I seriously doubt you do."

"I promise you I really do. I know exactly what you are going through."

"Are you an alcoholic as well?"

"No, but I do have an addiction."

"Really? So what are you addicted to? You're not one of these arseholes who try to equate addiction to drink and hard drugs with being addicted to chocolate or something else non life-threatening, are you?"

"No, not at all. My addiction is very serious indeed and, I must say, very life-threatening."

"So what are you addicted to then? I must say, you don't look like a junkie and actually appear quite well. Impeccably dressed too with that fancy designer suit of yours. I think you're full of shit."

"You wouldn't understand."

"Try me."

"No, honestly. It's nothing for you to concern yourself about."

"Seriously, fuckin' try me!"

"Okay then. If you must know, my addiction is to...blood."

"Blood?! How does that work then?"

"I need blood to survive. Without it I will perish."

"Are you fuckin' serious? We all need blood to survive! You talk some shit, I'll give you that."

"I don't mean our own blood. I mean the blood of other people. If I don't get it regularly it will kill me."

"You mean like donors?"

"In a manner of speaking."

"Were you in an accident or a car crash or something and you need blood from donors to keep you alive?"

Augustus raised his glass and knocked back his whiskey.

"Look, Stevie. I don't really expect you to understand fully, but for want of a better word I am a vampire and I have been around now for a very, very long time indeed. I'm addicted to the blood of others. It is my life source. I need it. I crave it. Just like you presumably crave for your dreaded alcohol. In many ways we are very similar. Both addicts. It's just our methods of feeding our insatiable appetites differ somewhat. Yours legal, mine illegal."

A long pause. A wide-mouthed Stevie eventually broke the silence.

"First up. I might be a cunt but I'm not a stupid cunt. Seriously. Fuck away off with your silly, childish shit. I'm not that drunk, for fuck's sake!"

Augustus laughed loudly.

"I promise you, Stevie, it's all completely true. I could actually do with a good blood binge right now, to be honest. Fancy coming out with me later on for a kill?"

"Ha ha, very funny, Mr 'Salem's Lot."

"I'm not joking."

"Neither am I. Well then, tell me this, Count Duckula. If you really are a vampire then how come you're in this bar when it is still broad daylight outside? And I could see your reflection clearly in that mirror in the toilet earlier too!"

"We're not afraid of crucifixes or garlic and don't sprout sharp fangs either! That's all just Hollywood rubbish you see in films. This isn't Buffy, you know. We are very real though. An ancient people whom originated in Eastern Europe back in the old days."

"Bullshit!"

"It's not bullshit, as you so crudely put it. Look, Stevie, why don't we have a few more drinks here and then later on, when it's dark, you can come along with me as I search for some new prey. I'll make it worth your while. I might even bestow upon you the honour of joining our very special and undying ranks. How would you like that? You'd become a new person altogether, your addiction to alcohol completely removed for good, albeit replaced with a new and much more satisfying one. I might even invite you to one of my blood orgies to meet a few friends of mine who I'm sure you'd like. You'd live forever. What do you reckon, Stevie? Does the promise of eternal life not tempt you?"

Another pause. This time even longer. The inebriated former call centre agent then spoke.

"I'll go with you if you buy a few more rounds here and lend me fifty quid to get more drink later."

Augustus smiled smugly.

"It's a deal."

The two men, one much drunker than the other, shook hands.

***

Stevie and his new found friend shared a few more drinks and laughs. There was no more tension between them, both now completely comfortable in each other's company. They left Hunter's bar before 8pm, just as it was beginning to pack up with more goth kids and students, leaving the warmth and friendly atmosphere of the Belfast pub and disappearing into the chilly winter's moonlit night. The snow was falling quite heavily as they headed up the Lisburn Road on a brand new adventure together. Stevie lit up a cigarette and drunkenly laughed to himself as his new pal waited on him smiling knowingly.

The former child magician was never seen by his family or friends again.

THE BEAST BENEATH (or I WAS A TEENAGE ALCOHOLIC)

'Of all the creatures, man is the most detestable. Of the entire brood, he is the one that possesses malice. He is the only creature that inflicts pain for sport, knowing it to be pain. The fact that man knows right from wrong proves his intellectual superiority to the other creatures; but the fact that he can do wrong proves his moral inferiority to any creature that cannot.'
(Mark Twain)

'As my story drew to a close, I realised I was the villain all along.'
(Joseph Gordon-Levitt)

Part One: THE PEN IS MIGHTIER THAN THE SWORD

June 1996

My memory returned to me not that long ago, although the concept of time, in the common understanding of it, has long since left my being. For what had felt like a very long period indeed, I had no recollection whatsoever of who or what I was. I was merely existing and surviving through basic animal instinct and intuition.

I was a human being once. In the regular sense of the word, that is. My ordeal, what I have been through, for what must have been many, many months, or even years, has evolved me greatly, and not in a very pleasant way either. I am more monster than man, but, for me, most men are monsters anyway, so I'm in familiar company. I was greatly wronged for quite some time, all culminating in the mess I find myself in now. However, as the old saying goes, vengeance is a dish best served chilled, and mine was indeed chilling and bloody.

I remember thinking at the time that I would take great care and pleasure in the brutal torture, mutilation and killing of my tormentors, in highly creative ways, as I can be quite the artiste, you know. The last thing I wanted them to remember was unearthly, incomprehensible pain and the sound of my laughter alongside their own terrified screams, pleading for mercy. As I said, I am now more beast than human, but perhaps this spiteful and violent streak has always resided deep within me, somewhat sadistically begging to be awakened and acted out in this profoundly nefarious, unforgiving world of men.

It all began in October of 1993 when I got my first ever proper adult job at the tender age of seventeen. Yea, I was seventeen, and a rather immature seventeen at that. The previous summer I had gotten the results of my all-important GCSEs exams and I'd pretty much fucked them right up, gaining weak passes or outright fails in the seven subjects I had chosen. Although I had showed some promise at an early age, by the time I had arrived at my mid-to-late teens I was more interested in football (or 'foozeball' as my soccer-hating mate Frank used to call it), girls, underage drinking and dabbling in recreational narcotics such as weed and LSD. I once heard a quote by Oscar Wilde where he stated something along the lines of youth being wasted on the young. Well, by fuck, that was most definitely the case with me. I even remember my mother catching me looking at football and porno mags hidden within my school text books when I should have been revising from them.

So, as previously mentioned, I inevitably made a right bollocks of my GCSEs, not even getting the required grades to go back to school and study for my A Levels and perhaps even make it to university after that. Not knowing which important life move to make next - and not really giving a proper shit either, as some of my mates of the time were a bit older than me and already out working and making hedonistic weekend-funding cash, with me wanting a piece of the action - I enrolled in Belfast's Castlereagh College School of Printing, an establishment which eventually set me up with my first paid job (not counting my childhood paper rounds) at Collage Litho Plates, a pre-press printing firm, following in my deceased father's footsteps in the trade. Such a small, grubby, uninviting, horrid, windowless, depressing little shithole it was too. And I say paid job, but the fuckers never actually paid me a single penny for any of my back-breaking laborious toils there. I was hired by them on one of those awful government YTP schemes, where innocent youths are paid a measly £37.50 (including travel expenses) per week on the agreement that they received proper training and an apprenticeship. Those 'Youth Training Programmes' were indeed legalised forms of slavery, the bastards! Totally cuntish behaviour in the exploitation of the young. May their wicked consciences plague them for the rest of their living days. If I haven't butchered and slaughtered them first, that is, of course. It was around the time of my first few months of gainful employment at Collage Shithole Plates, that I made the informed and pleasing-at-the-time decision to get more involved in hardcore drug-taking (ie. Ecstasy, Es, those little white doves, 'rhubarbs and custards' etc) and all-night raving/weekend-long partying. This was a decision which invariably had its ups and downs, or highs and lows as more professional-sounding so-called experts might call it. And, along with my ever-growing alcoholism, it turned me into a less than model and grateful employee.

But so fucking what?! I was, and still am in many ways, I guess, an immature and directionless kid that didn't deserve their awful treatment of me, which starting with verbal and physical bullying and culminated in my little 'accident'. Yea, that fucking so-called accident. I'll come to that soon enough though.

Collage Litho Plates was a colour proofing/printing firm founded in the 1960s (like, who even really cares?!) in the Shore Row area of Belfast by it's owner and general overall commander-in-chief, Bert Hamilton (cunt!). It was, and still is, a torrid little hellhole that can be found at the bottom of the humble and quiet Linfield Street, close to the old linen mill and industrial estate, and beside the Presbyterian church. Whilst working there, I was trained up as a plate-maker and proofer, which is essentially dealing with the early stages of the printing processes, before any print job makes it to the final press and run. Hey, look, it's all boring technical stuff and pointless exposition, so I'm just going to leave it at that and concentrate on the main story, which is much more interesting anyway. You'll understand in due course once we get to all those lovely gory details.

I will, however, mention my old bedsit which I moved into on Botanic Avenue near the Stranmillis area of South Belfast, walking distance from work, which was handy. I moved into it in '94 and really enjoyed my time there, despite my tiny homestead's relative compactness. Well, at least it was clean. Most of the time anyway. Certainly not in the aftermath of my friends and I's weekend long, drink and drug-induced parties, with ash and empties strewn everywhere in some sort of modern art masterpiece of debauchery. Oh, and by the way, back when I was human, our weekends used to run from Thursday nights right up until the early hours of Monday morning. Sometimes they would even begin on a Wednesday night, depending on the general mood and financial situation. Naturally, Mondays to Wednesdays in work were set aside for the much-needed recovery and recuperation period from the excessive taking of toxins - some legal, some very illegal.

A typical weekend would start with the 'Thursday Night Club' in my mate John Brown's roof-space attic. Nothing spectacular at this point really, just a few joints and a clatter of tins of beer whilst John would spin a few tunes on his turntables, budding bedroom DJ that he was. I would usually get home at around midnight to make it into Collage

Wankstain Plates not-so-fit for work the next morning. Friday nights would be spent in a local bar and/or nightclub and Saturdays entailed drinking at a pub in town all day (the 'Saturday Club') before heading off to one of the big rave super-clubs, like the Network or Xanadu, for a spot of all-night dancing, revelling, and, of course, binge-drinking and substance abuse. We always ended up in a house party in the early hours of a Sunday after kicking out time at said club, so the entirety of the good Lord's day and night would be spent there with more of the same sort of immoral, sinful behaviour. In many ways, in retrospect, they really were some of the best of times. I couldn't do it again though. Not in my current monstrous state anyway, but more on that later.

As my hangovers and poor performance in the workplace got worse, so did the bullying and abuse there. Aside from the back-breakingly heavy and physical (and many times probably illegal!) work/slavery, I was regularly taunted and made fun of. The usual names I would be called were variations on the always charming and delightful 'useless cunt', 'stupid, ugly bastard', 'waste of a good wank' and 'skinny, dying-looking spastic'. Physical violence, in the form of slaps and punches to the face soon ensued whenever I fucked up printing jobs and I was even once mocked and teased whenever one of my best friends committed suicide by hanging, my usual tormentors, like Jon the van driver, Ken James and Terry Haughey, even deliberately trying to block me getting a day off for his funeral out of sheer spiteful nastiness. Yes, what a lovely place Collage Fuckface Plates was and probably still is. To be completely fair though, there were some quite nice and decent people who worked there too, like the very amiable Paul McCrory, for example, but the good were always overshadowed by the bad and the brutish, a blind eye forever being turned by senior management, including Bert Hamilton's second-in-command, the vile, hideous Ian Graham, another uber-cunt who quite literally resembled a ginger-haired, mustachioed farmyard pig, the fat fuck! This excuse for a man was also one of my main banes, the obese bundle of turd giving the other bullying ballbags the green light to do and say what they wanted to me.

But enough of all this tedious, although perhaps relevant, back story. Let's now move on to the details of my little 'accident'.

Part Two: WE ARE ALL IN THE GUTTER, BUT SOME OF US ARE LOOKING UP AT THE STARS

My usual weekly hours of labour at Collage Cuntwaffle Plates were from 8am until 4pm, Mondays to Fridays, with any overtime paid at a 'time and a half' rate. Overtime was forced on the staff, by the way, and I am rather surprised that they even paid the union rate for it, going by Bert Hamilton's past track record of not abiding by regulations and paying his apprentices pittance. Seriously, Ebenezer Scrooge has fuck all on this bastard! Heck, he even one time refused to pay a guy for coming in for eight long hours on a Sunday (which should have been paid at double time according to union laws), due to the lad accidentally ruining the job. I guess the union was just pretty useless and powerless in thon place.

One Thursday afternoon in late '95, I was informed by Ian 'ginger Jabba the Hutt' Graham that I was needed to work overtime late into the night so the job would be ready for the customer first thing the next morning. I refused initially, panicked and horrified at the thought of missing this week's 'Thursday Night Club' with my compadres of life and existentialist fulfillment. But Ian 'Donkey-fucker' Graham, and some of my other scourges, browbeat, humiliated and blackmailed me into agreeing to it.

The job in question was to be the proofing (a form of printing) of a load of toothpaste packs on the big press in the back room. The plates (which lithographic printing was done from) would not be ready from Marty and Robert in the planning department until around 5pm, after Alan and Rory in the scanning room had made a right balls up, leading to the delay. I would be required to proof the packs on the press as soon as the plates were ready, printing them in the four process colours of cyan, magenta, yellow and black, and two extra colours, a shade of pink and a blue. Motherfuckers! I was fuming and knew I would end up having to stay in that horrible place until around 2am, most definitely missing the John Brown-hosted Thursday evening festivities. And to make matters much worse, I already had one seriously stinking hangover to deal with, as Robbie Snake and I had been out on the lash the night before trying to pull girls in a shite bar/nightclub known as the Chicago Dance Factory. I was still feeling rough as a badger's arse and just wanted to either get a cure with my friends or go straight home to bed. Probably the cure though, now that I think about it.

When the time came to begin the job, my mind was a mess of craving for drink and frustration at being forced to stay. Those other two bastards, Bert and Ian, were still in the building, claiming to be going over some paperwork in Bert's orifice, I mean office, but in reality were most likely polishing off a bottle of whiskey or four, while his hapless Great Dane dog looked on in uninterested boredom, the dumb animal. Yea, old Bert was well fond of a drink or ten and his breath regularly reeked of the stuff in the mornings, alongside his usual pipe smoke. Just like my own did with the booze on many occasions, I guess. But those king shits had an absolute cheek and gall to harass me about my drinking and label me an alcoholic, the hypocrites!

Those huge and powerful rollers on the press were spinning and mixing the ink at a great and vigorous pace. While they applied the ink to the image on the metal plate, the large steel cylinder blanket took an impression and redistributed it onto the blank card packages, one at a time, as I loaded them up by hand, ensuring at the same time everything on the machine was kept cool and damp. Despite my tiredness, hungover-ness and general pissed off-ness, the first four colours went on reasonably well. The cyan, although a little light at first, soon got up to weight. The magenta went on a treat, surprisingly, and yellow is usually one of the easiest colours to get up to density anyway. The black was a piece of piss, as it was only needed for some outlining and lettering, so I whacked that out in no time at all. The real problems began to arise with the extra colours.

I began with the pink, which was a real fucker to mix from the outset. As my temper was starting to fray with an angry expediency, I eventually got the colour to a passable and usable shade before using the palate knives to spread it evenly on the wildly turning rollers. Up and down the flat bed press went, while I loaded up blank sheets of card to get the pink up to a final and acceptable weight before using on the proper prints. I remember vividly, almost in slow motion and black and white - like some sort of old silent film - the details of the following life-changing carnage.

Just as I was very close to reaching the correct level of this difficult pink, I added some more ink onto the rollers, just enough I thought. But when I inserted the next piece of card into the correct compartment of the press, whenever it returned to me it was way over in density. My patience was at its end and I threw a violent strop, screaming "FUCK OFF!" at the top of my voice and kicking the underside of the steel press, hurting my left foot badly and possibly breaking a toe into the bargain. I was raging and shaking, in a combination of exhaustion, hunger and sheer frustration, but realised that I had to try and keep a cool head and finish the job at hand so I could head home as soon as humanly possible and have a few well deserved beers and maybe even a 'barrack buster' of three litre cheap and nasty cider. My terrible accident and series of unspeakable misfortune began when I tried to remove some of the ink from the rollers - manually switching them off and inserting a blank sheet of card into them, circulating it around by hand and removing it when it was felt enough ink was removed. A crude method, yes, but one that would usually suffice. Ninety-nine percent of the time anyway. My problem arose therein when, in my state of fluster and self-induced mania, I forget to switch the rollers off before embarking on my ink removal operation. It all happened very quickly really. For that split second when I first entered the piece of white card into those pounding, wielding, twisting and turning rollers, I actualised in my mind that I had just made a huge mistake.

The metallic machine monsters violently jerked and pulled me into their whirling netherworld of agony alongside the piece of card. My adrenalin was pumping as fast as those mother-fucking rollers and instinctively, as it was attempting to pull me right in, I managed to snatch my already bloodied and damaged left hand out and grab onto the side of the press. But it was too late for my right hand and arm. And my face too.

My blood, something similar to one of the colours I had once mixed in that very same room in Collage Asshole Plates, was now part of the pink ink mix on those god-awful rollers, giving it a deep and dark crimson-like texture. I somehow doubt the customer would have been happy with this now new shade of pink and would most definitely have returned the job for a reprint. I was on the ground beside the mammoth proofing press in a state semi-consciousness. My detached, bloodied and meshed up right arm was lying neatly beside me on my right side, just under the front of the press. It really is such a strange and fascinating sight to look upon one of your own limbs just after it has been severed and it is an image that shall be forever etched into my memory. The blood, mixed in with the pink ink, was everywhere around me. All over the floor, walls and press and I was lying in a pool of it myself. Tendons and little lumps of flesh were scattered all about my immediate vicinity. My face was messed up badly as well after the rollers had tried to drag it through. The right side of it had been partially squashed by those daunting spinning cylinders. My eye on the same side was pulled out and squashed like a grape and eaten up inside the great mechanism. Part of my nose had been removed also, large clumps of my hair yanked out, my right ear sliced off, and my lips and many of my teeth no longer appeared to exist either, all forever lost in a world of industrial machinery.

I was in a right royal mess and it wasn't long before I passed out completely.

***

The next things I remember were the sounds of voices and the sensation of being dragged somewhere. My thinking was almost totally clouded and I really did not know what was going on at all, but I do have some vague recollection of something really bad having just happened. My main senses were obviously highly impaired. It was all like some sort of awful nightmare.

Two mature and male voices were audible, both strangely familiar. One was deep and husky, like that of a long-time smoker of a pipe. The other was squeaky, shrill and annoying.

Voice one, husky smoker, was the first I heard clearly after only catching mumblings as my semi-conscious state gradually returned:

"We've got to get rid of this body. For fuck's sake compose yourself, man. This has all been one terrible accident, but there's nothing we can do for the poor lad now. And if we don't think and act now by cleaning up this unholy mess, we're going to be in a lot of serious trouble with the law and possibly even facing jail time due to some sort of industrial negligence charge or the like. And then who would employ you? How would you afford to pay that mortgage and flashy sports car of yours? By fuck, that mad wife of yours would divorce you in a millisecond and then what would you do, eh? Come on, man, let's clean this up and stick to the story and do the right thing for all concerned. God help me, if I could I would never have let this happen, but it's way to late for the boy now. We need to sort this out, pronto!"

The squeaky shrill voice spoke next, his words trembling slightly and nervous: "Fuck me, Bert. This is awful. I know he was a wanker and a waster but he didn't deserve this. Stupid cunt was probably drunk or spaced out on the job again. His own fault. One silly wee boy."

"That's right! It was the stupid little fucker's own fault and we can't blame ourselves, man. But we need to do what is right by ourselves and the company now. This is bad, I'll admit it, but we can fix it," stated husky smoker.

"Fuck. We'll just have to tell the peelers he disappeared from the place when he should have been here working and finishing that job. Say he's probably went off on one of his benders again somewhere. Seems a pretty realistic story anyway given his past form. C'mon, let's get this over and done with and get cleaned up."

"Exactly, man. This can easily be explained away to the coppers. Come on over here and help me lift the body."

I was being dragged and pulled again by the two men who owned the voices. I believe I was in a state of extreme shock and delirium at the time, out of my mind by natural causes for a change. I heard the clattering and banging of some sort of thick iron-like lid being lifted next and the dripping water of toilets and sinks. Squeaky shrill was mumbling incoherently and in a bit of a state now.

Husky smoker was firm and assertive: "For fuck's sake, pull yourself together, man. Help me dump this body down here and then all we have to do is get that god damned proofing room cleaned up and no-one will be any the wiser! Come on, man!"

And with that simple command, those two despicable cunts tossed my mashed up body into the toilet sewers below Collage Litho Plates and closed the lid firmly back on it, leaving what was left of me in a pitch black hell of darkness and funk.

***

I can remember very little of the following weeks and months and soon lost track of any sense of time completely. What I do know is this: the eyesight in my one remaining eye eventually returned in full and became accustomed to my dark surroundings. My bleeding stopped at some point and my wounds healed, in a manner of speaking, although not fully and probably never will. During my recovery over what I can only guess has been several months, I have survived down here in some sort of animalistic, base demeanour. Although very weak at first, my strength has slowly returned. My brief trains of sane thinking are of my mother and sisters and, strangely, a pop song that I once quite liked by a Canadian rock band named the Crash Test Dummies. The lyrics of their song, *God Shuffled His Feet*, would oft randomly run though my head:

'The people sipped their wine,
And what with God there, they asked him questions,
Like: do you have to eat,
Or get your hair cut in Heaven?
And if your eye got poked out in this life,
Would it be waiting up in Heaven with your wife?

So He said:"Once there was a boy,
Who woke up with blue hair.
To him it was a joy,
Until he ran out into the warm air.
He thought of how his friends would come to see;
And would they laugh, or had he got some strange disease?'

It was all very peculiar and, in addition, I have vague recollections of my diet consisting of the piss and faeces that was regularly flushed into my new home from above. Who knows what other bodily fluids were alongside this awful human wastage! I also ingested many industrial chemicals during my time here. Chemical wastage which, just like myself, had been ditched down here by my former co-employees, for a firm which never really was one for health and safety in the past anyway. To add to this, I also have a memory of getting some painfully bad stomach cramps after feasting on slippery, jelly-like frogspawn once or twice. Small animals, like rats, other rodent life forms and insects, were also devoured during my time down here and I even once ate a wild cat live, ripping off it ears with my abomination of a disfigured mouth at first, while it squealed and scratched at me in a panicked frenzy, before I suffocated the feline between my naked thighs and munched the rest of it down, the eyes and paws a particularly tasty delicacy.

As my mind eventually returned amidst the horrific odours and disgusting sewage of my new environment, over those horribly long days of permanent darkness, I soon became even more embittered and full of a raging, terrible anger. I had realised what had happened to me and who had disposed of me to my personal Hades and I longed to set the record straight once and for all, with my twisted revenge truly unforgettable and devastating to all concerned. I had a rough plan mapped out in my mind, so all I had to do was be vigilant, patient and wait for the right time. Sweet vengeance in Biblical proportions would be mine indeed, I mused.

Part Three: AN EYE FOR AN EYE, A TOOTH FOR A TOOTH

On the night of our final reckoning, Bert Hamilton and Ian Graham were having one of their usual drinking sessions in Bert's office, the smug bastards. Before setting off on my mission, I briefly napped, leaping upright from a curious dream about a colour not on any known spectrum or scale. It was the colour of insanity mixed with bloodlust and sadness. I missed my mother and sisters badly, but how can I ever let them see me like this? Perhaps they are better off believing I am dead.

Although I could hear both of those hateful old men from a distance if I sat at a certain point in the underground, I made one of my rare visits to the street outside from the back entrance to the sewer, which led onto an adjoining street, undetected by any members of the public. I did this to make sure that my victims' cars were parked outside the building, which they were, my spying of Ian's jazzy black sports car first of all, followed by Bert's golden Mercedes. Fuck, that auld fucker Bert was like a real-life version of Monty Burns from *The Simpsons*, I pondered to myself before slipping quietly back into the sewer.

I armed myself with crude weapons, into and over my only remaining arm and hand - an old red 'Belfast' brick, a elongated and sharpened shard of glass and some electrical cable which I had recently found - and entered College Litho Plates through the same way in which I had last left it - through the closed-over sewer entrance in the toilets.

Another lyric from that Crash Test Dummies song suddenly popped into my head as I crawled up into the company bathroom:

> 'The people sat waiting,
> Out on their blankets in the garden,
> But God said nothing.
> So someone asked Him: "I beg your pardon:
> I'm not quite clear about what you just spoke,
> Was that a parable, or a very subtle joke?"'

The bright lighting in the toilet took a while to get accustomed to, but once I did the first sight I happened upon was a truly tragic one: the terrifying, dejected face of a madman, a monster, not unlike one from the type of horror films I used to enjoy so much as a kid. This pathetic creature stared back me with a great despondency and sadness. Its naked flesh was a jaundiced yellow in colour, with huge blotches and sores simmering with cream puss all over its wretched, skinny failing body, large blue veins pulsing outwards, and its head hair all patchy and white. The creature seemed to be in all sorts of pain. A single tear fell from its one and only eye.

I stepped away from the bathroom looking glass and made my way, as quietly as possible, to Bert's upstairs office beside the main admin area.

My strength, although reasonably strong considering all I had been through, might not have been enough to overpower two fully fit, for their age anyway, middle-aged men, so I knew I had to summon something from deep within as I clambered up those wooden stairs. I had to channel all that hatred and anger into something special to enable the carrying out of my brutal acts, and that is exactly what I did.

"Hey, fuckwits. Remember me?" I struggled to slur from my lipless mouth as I clambered through Bert's office door, clocking him first, puffing away on his old pipe with a certain degree of contented condescending glee.

The two men stopped what they were doing immediately and stared at me with looks of true revulsion and shock embalmed on their drunkenly reddened faces. Bert's dopey dog, 'Goldie', was asleep underneath its master's desk, as it so often did.

I stumbled across the office towards them with my only arm placed behind my back, hiding my tools of destruction.

"Are you okay, son?" a clearly on-edge Bert Hamilton asked.

"Let me call you an ambulance," added that fat asshole, Ian.

"Don't fucking bother, pricks," I relayed in my contorted, strange-to-hear voice.

Bert set down his Sherlock Holmes-style pipe in the large wooden ashtray on his desk and moved from behind it to beside where Ian was, as I neared on them, almost stumbling as I did. As Bert stood beside his second-in-command, the duo seemed frozen and aghast in terror at what was standing before them.

"Oh my god. What in the hell happened to you, son?" inquired the clearly lying Bert.

An awkward pause.

"Look at the state of you, boy," added my horrified former boss.

"You know fine well what happened to me, you lying devious bastards. Look at me! Fucking look at me! You did this to me! And all to save yourselves a miserly few quid. You evil old fuckers! You've turned me into some sort of disgusting beast creature. I am not a monster though. I am a human being! I'm just a kid! I had my whole life in front of me and now look at me?! I'm a fucking mess because of you! I will NEVER forgive you for this!" I screamed at the top of my distorted larynx.

Single swift and powerful blows to the tops of their skulls with the red brick were enough to knock the two already intoxicated men out, felling them to the office floor.

That stupid mutt, Goldie, wakened at all the commotion and yelped and barked in my direction. The glass shard through the top of the animal's cranium was enough to silence it for good. After crashing the brick onto the men's heads a few more times to make sure they were out cold, I began my real work on this duo of despicable cunts.

Ian Graham was to be first for the special and skilled treatment.

Delicately and masterfully using the shard of glass on him, I sliced up and peeled off his obese face with that silly moustache on it, leaving nothing but blistering red flesh and pumping veins, rendering him virtually unrecognisable. Definitely an improvement. I was remarkably calm throughout the whole process, but a slight and brief twinge of anger resulted in me driving the shard directly through his right eye.

'And if your eye got poked out in this life,
Would it be waiting up in Heaven with your wife?'

When he appeared to come around a little, muttering gibberish which resulted in little bubbles of blood rising up from the hole that used to be his mouth, I stuck my makeshift blade deep into his grossly overweight abdomen, left it in for while before removing it slowly (for added tortuous pain effect) and then proceeded to scalp the fucker's fat head. Once finished, I gently removed the top of his dome by his ginger locks, leaving the purple-grey coloured brain matter exposed, a few little trickles of blood running down to where his face used to be. A fittingly awful end for an truly awful person.

Now it was time to give the bossman himself his just desserts.

With my one arm, I dragged his near lifeless body away with me, just like he and his co-conspirator had once done with my good self. As I pulled him down the wooden stairs of College Revenge Plates, I made sure the back of his head banged off every single step on the way down. When we reached the toilets and entrance to the sewer, I could hear him mumbling what I reckoned was some sort of apology and pleadings for mercy. But I was resolute in my determination for what had to be done and there was no way in the world I was going to fall for a sob story at this point. Not a fuckin' chance of it! To fuck the old bastard up properly, I had to use all of my strength to lift up the massively heavy steel lid of the sewer entrance and crash it off his skull. Auld Bert's head hit the ground with an squeamish thud and crunch, rendering him knocked out again, but still breathing slightly.

Then I truly and properly went to town on him, weaving the electric cable into his body, starting with his scrotum sack, up through his groin, back down though his stomach, into the other limbs and parts of his torso, before finally out through his throat and into the right eye socket, forcing the eye itself to drop out slightly before I had to slice the rest of it off completely.

'And if your eye got poked out in this life...'

I was the fucking puppet master now and for my grand finale, I also scalped my old boss as well, and bit off his tongue with one large bite of what was remaining of my own mouth. I chewed on it for a while before swallowing it down. It tasted and felt good. With my work now over, I pulled the remainder of Bert Hamilton into the sewer with me and shut the lid. The rest of his remains would keep me going food-wise for about a week, I thought, but after that I would have to go back to my old dietary habits of rat and cat mixed with chemicals, piss and shit. Maybe even try a little more frogspawn again sometime.

***

I have yet to be apprehended for my crimes on that night and still reside in that spacious sewer I now call my home. I believe I lost the final remnants of my humanity on that fateful night of revenge in my former workplace. I don't really know what I am now. Some sort of indescribable 'It', I suppose. Life can be rather boring and tedious down here for the most part and I still dearly miss my mother and sisters. Maybe I will go and visit them some day before handing myself into the police and confessing to my wretched acts, but they will not like what they would see.

On a more positive note, I haven't touched a drop of alcohol or dropped a pill in quite some time now, so every cloud really does have a silver lining. More importantly, I have exacted my retribution on my main tormentors from the past. Perhaps I might even go after the other ones some day. Maybe. Maybe not. You know, when they used to all abuse me in the old days, they would often retort that they were not laughing at me, but laughing with me, to cover their own backs. What utter bollocks! They are all just small people, with tiny ideas on life in their petty and narrow minds. I had the last laugh in the end.

So, for the meantime, I am feeling rather contented and absolved.

Ego sum absolutus.

HARVEST

'This was black magic, and it was easy to use. Easy and fun. Like Legos.' (Jim Butcher)

The masked entity prepared its unholy altar. A creature of darkness whom once took human form, seemingly aeons ago if measured in the trivial terms that mankind attests to in his vain and limited scope. Very little is known of this timeless being, although in rare whispered and knowing circles it is reckoned that as a man some centuries ago, he once falsely incriminated a certain well thought of carpenter for the toll of a measly bag of silver coins. Before this, and after, the entity had been, and would be known by, many other titles; Baal, Titivillus, Azazal, Beliar, Herne the Hunter being just some of the many designations presented to this prince of the underworld.

The altar was located in a mostly unknown cave, deep under a picturesque hilly area in the city of Belfast in twenty-first century Northern Ireland. A humble at times land, but one cursed and soaked with the blood of its ancestors - combatants and fools in a protracted tribal war between two related sects, fighting against their neighbours in the name of the same Judeo-Christian God. Lucifer himself must have really chuckled at that one. The lives of the innocent suffered most at the hands of the evil men do.

A circle of salt was formed around the altar. Black candles were lit on the long rotting wooden table in the dripping and cold chamber, surrounded by the cunning being's grimoire of incantations, ancient crystals, reverse talismans, and ceremonial blade. Many insects of the earth, such as beetles, woodlouse', millipedes and spiders scuttled over and around the wood. The entity - let's call it a Soul Devourer - was covered in its liturgical deep red robes and cloak, and had with it a cumbersome sack, one which moved and jerked oddly, making strange inhuman screeching sounds at the same time.

The contents of the sack - a domestic tomcat, a Jack Russell terrier, a cockerel and a bird of the air (a crow) - were emptied forthwith onto the decrepit, death-smelling table, fighting and clawing at each other in sheer panic and desperation, the poor animals covered in bloodied scrapes and gashes resulting from their blind fight with each other for survival. One of the front legs of the cat had almost been ripped from its body, hanging on by a tendril, while the dog's left eye was now removed from the socket, a reddened soaking hole in its place. The messed up crow was dazed and confused, as the cockerel stumbled while trying to walk on broken limbs. Hairs and feathers filled the air, as dark bodily fluids from the four beasts soaked the altar, all the while as they clawed and pecked in disorientated desperation, almost comically if the circumstances were not so gravely depraved.

The Soul Devourer calmly and routinely clutched each dumb, but yet generally harmless, living organism in turn by the neck and removed each of their heads swiftly with the razor sharp ceremonial dagger, lopping them towards the centre of the makeshift altar whilst dropping the torsos on the ground at first, before picking them up at the end of the slaughter and setting them beside the rest of the remains on the table. As it lay on the putrid altar of sin, the decapitated body of the cockerel twitched somewhat due to its now failing internal neural networks.

After the macabre sacrifice to its immediate superiors and ultimate Master, the being known as the Soul Devourer turned its attention to the grimoire book and the recitation of some of the rites contained within, inked in what is believed by some to be human blood. The diabolical chant performed was not of this celestial sphere and indeed belonged only to a ghastly and terrible region of another dimension altogether - that of the fiery lake of burning sulphur and the second death, wherein beholds a never ceasing wailing and gnashing of teeth.

At the completion of the ritual, the strange figure extinguished the black candles and made haste for the exit of the cave and into the surrounding misty early morning woods ahead, making tracks to the area where its superiors had just revealed would contain its long-craved after reward - a nourishing feast indeed, and a true human sacrifice to be offered up with glee.

The Cruel and Forbidden Ones would be most pleased.

***

Mark enjoyed jogging a lot. It helped clear his head and essentially keep him sane. There was a lot of stigma still attached to mental illness in Northern Ireland, so there was no way in the world that he was ever going to admit to Joe Public that he had recently been diagnosed with bipolar disorder. Not a chance of it, he reckoned. And that's if he was even really mentally ill in the first place, as that condescending psychiatrist had concluded. They love to put labels on people, stick them in a box and throw a load of happy pills down their gullets until they don't know what day it is, or what planet they're on. Control, that's what it was all about, mused Mark, as he stepped up his pace on the Upper Crumlin Road and onto the Horse Shoe Bend.

Mark hadn't taken his medication in weeks and, if truth be told, was still arrogantly in denial of Dr. Rainey's medical opinion of what he suffered from. On a generous day he would perhaps offer the suggestion that what he really suffered from was in fact *drug-induced* bipolar, as the delusions and deep depression quite often followed an intense weed smoking session. He didn't smoke quite as much now anyway, certainly nowhere near as much as he would have in his teenage years and twenties, which was basically all day, every day, but now at thirty-two years of age he felt he no longer needed it as much and had somewhat grown out of the phase. Those couple of enforced stays at Knockbracken mental health facility had certainly given him food for thought regarding his lifestyle too. That, and a few nervous breakdowns. Deep down, however, in some remote back corner of his very essence, Mark knew rightly that he wasn't well and the medical professionals were right. He just simply could not admit it. But running at the crack of dawn, when all was serene and most mere mortals where still enjoying the slumber of the hard-worked and downtrodden, was the time of day Mark enjoyed most. When he could almost touch and feel his peace of mind, and where the manic racing brain could be tamed for a little while.

The Cavehill area of North Belfast has, in recent times, been rather popular with outdoorsy sporting types - hikers, cyclists, dog walkers (if that can be considered a sport), those ridiculous looking power walkers who move like they've soiled themselves, and, of course, the joggers like Mark Tate. Oh, and let us not forget the teenage drinkers also, who congregate in the region at the weekends, their rave music pumping obnoxiously loud for all and sundry nearby to be deafened by.

The region itself could be best described as a wooded hill that the locals have always claimed to be a mountain. But it's not a mountain, it's a big hill at best. Anyway, the peak of the summit is the rocky 'Napoleon's Nose', a cliff of sorts which is host to, it must be said, the most splendid view imaginable, which takes in most of East Belfast, Belfast harbour, Newtownabbey, and to the right, Newcastle, County Down and the Mountains of Mourne sweeping down to the sea. On a really good day you can even see Scotland across the lough and to the direct left of Napoleon's Nose is Belfast Zoo with all its lions and tigers and bears, oh my. On the cliff face are a couple of caves and the foot of the cliff leads into more woodland, eventually running down into the nineteenth century-built Belfast Castle and its grounds. The whole area is truly beauteous and awe-inspiring and certainly one of the jewels in Belfast's oft-troubled crown. Rumours had always abounded though of the general terrain being historically host to druid activity and even that of the Dark Arts. The great scenery, however, was one of the other main reasons that Mark enjoyed running there.

It was particularly mild early spring morning, with the dew moistening the majority of the surroundings and Mark's breath was visible as he huffed and puffed his way onto the Hightown Road and towards the side entrance to the now council-run Cavehill Country Park. It was shortly after 7.30am so the place was still be very much unpopulated, something which suited the runner perfectly.

Mark, who could certainly feel himself getting fitter and healthier with these morning exercises, rounded the entrance to the Cavehill Country Park, breezed past the car park and the picnic tables and on down the pathway which would eventually lead him to the main hill and wooded areas. The cows in the fields beside the dirt track where he moved watched him with a vague, casual disinterest, obviously now well used to the sight of human life, in all its ridiculous forms, entering their domain. A few rays of sunlight were trying to creep through the morning mist like inter-dimensional alien burglars trying to break into our universe.

The dusty path led downhill slightly, eventually taking Mark to the usual crossroads he had approached many mornings before. He had the choice of going left and up the Cavehill, which would soon take him to the top, the wondrous view, and onto the Napoleon's Nose, or take the right path, which would take him around the side of the mountain, past the quarry where a woman's body was found strangled and beaten some years prior, through some woodland and eventually onto the grounds of Belfast Castle. After a couple of minutes pause, to mainly catch his breath and stretch a bit, he decided upon taking the right hand path, the reasons being that the upward stretch to the top of the Cavehill was a tough one on the legs, feeling almost vertical at certain points, it wasn't much of a day to enjoy the view up there with the mist making it practically unseeable, and also he fancied the change from his usual route anyway. Once he reached the castle grounds, he could jog on down to the Antrim Road, take a right onto the North Circular Road, leading on to the Ballysillan Road, and then home for a shower and some breakfast.

It was a decision he would soon regret in the gravest of manners.

The wild horses in the field beside the country track Mark was now pacing on were playing and galloping away idly, beautiful creatures enjoying the morning and the full splendour of the natural world at its finest. They barely even noticed the jogger as he passed by them, but when he noticed them with their frivolous, innocent nature it brought a smile to his face.

An early rising dog walker was the only other human being Mark saw that day, as he paced past the old quarry at the side of the main hill, greeting the elderly man with the usual pleasantries, which were returned.

As the wooded region approached, the thirty-two year old stopped to catch his breath again. He was thirsty and was now regretting not bringing a bottle of water with him on his journey. He had no choice but to press on regardless and into the trees and forest which awaited him with a gaping mouth.

Birds chirped a pleasant song overhead whilst the surrounding trees and growth seemed to ooze with a living vibrancy. The spirit of the surrounding nature was filled with vitality. Mark felt good. He felt truly alive, at one with his environment and immersed in the feeling that he was living life the way it was truly intended. Although it was a feeling that would soon be cut short for him.

As he rounded a sharp bend on the dirt road he was treading on, Mark glimpsed something out of the corner of his left eye that he had never noticed before. Although he usually took the other route on the Cavehill during his morning runs, he knew the general area pretty well and had quite a few times taken the same path he was on now. Through the trees and overgrowth on his left side was a rather odd sight and one that gave him a feeling of deep disorientation. There was a house, a single-floored cottage, apparently derelict for some time. A dirty-looking place, perhaps a couple of hundred years old at least. Surely he could not have missed seeing this all the times he had been past the exact same area before, Mark thought to himself while at the same time filled with both curiosity and unease. The outside walls of the house were stone and had at one point in its past been painted white, but the paint had now faded greatly. There were two glassless windows with black curtains draped on the inside, an ancient-looking oak door at the front, a smoking chimney on top and all around and over it there was a mass of twisted moss and weeds. The area surrounding was now in complete silence. A stunned unnatural silence. The air had turned chilly, suddenly much colder than just before and upon impulsively checking his wristwatch Mark found to his confusion that the minutes and seconds hands were rotating backwards of their own accord, anti-clockwise. He felt nauseous and suspected he was becoming sick again. He had being doing great of late but now felt he was on the onset of another bipolar episode and maybe even a full breakdown. He contemplated that he could be suffering from some delusions again, whilst attempting to compose and steady his being through the controlled breathing exercises he had been taught at the 'nervous' hospital.

Sick or not, the house still seemed very real in his mind and was a conundrum Mark wanted to get to the bottom of, to at very least put the mystery in his mind to rest and feed his increasing nervous inquisitiveness. He put his hands briefly over his face, rustled his blonde hair, and decided to walk towards the mysterious house.

The damp oak door was slightly ajar and Mark now noticed some etchings on the front it - scrawlings carved in an peculiar language unbeknownst to him. A verse it seemed, a poem perhaps. A solitary black crow sat on the roof above the door in silence, its deviously dark eyes watching his every move, almost motionless, yet its glare almost piercing right through his body. The bird's eyes followed his every step as he opened the door and entered the hallway, while a feeling of impending doom rushed over his body. As Mark stepped into the house, a putrid stench of decaying death filtered into his nostrils, almost overcoming him.

The walls in the hallway were filthy, smeared in excrement and dirt. The floor was covered in dead leaves and other debris like the carcasses of birds and rodents, their bloodied and mashed up innards being gorged on hurriedly by insect life, scurrying and fighting with each other for the tastiest, most nourishing bits. It was almost as if this rancid place was a home to anti-nature, with death and negativity all around. In front of Mark there were doorless entrances to four rooms, two on each side. He walked into the first one on the left, now in some sort of trance of trepidation.

More of the same vile mess and corpses of birds and cats littered the ground, but on the crumbling once white-painted wall facing the doorway, there was a message for him, scribed in huge messily-written words. The words, it appeared, had been authored in blood:

IN NATURE THERE ARE NEITHER CONSEQUENCES OR REWARDS. ONLY PUNISHMENTS.

Below the writings was the image of an upside-down cross with a crudely drawn serpent wrapped around it, daubed in blood also. Bloodied human hand prints were also imprinted on the walls of this horrid room, with Mark noticing that blood seemed to be dripping from the right hand curtain at the window too. He went over to investigate more, transfixed with the horror show in front of him.

The jet black, thick silken drapes had more of the strange indecipherable letterings and symbols on them. Mark had never seen this form of language or written word before, but somehow he could sense that there was something very old and very unholy concerning everything about this wicked place. Was he sick and having some sort of awful hallucination - perhaps lying somewhere on the Cavehill, unconscious and dreaming a nightmare of intense horrors? He simply couldn't tell anymore but decided upon exiting this room to investigate the rest of the squalid surroundings.

Two of the other three rooms were quite similar to the first one he had witnessed - rotting death and sacrilegious graffiti - but the far room to the right, the last one Mark entered, was something different altogether. It was warm and almost welcoming. There was a lit open fire at the centre of the far wall, the source of the smoke coming from the chimney outdoors. The flames crackled and danced from the wood excitedly, like little fire sprites or imps and they seemed to be emitting a strange, though pleasant-smelling, perfume-like odour too. The ceiling and walls were covered in the most beautiful, if somewhat macabre and vivid, artwork, covering almost the entirety of them and depicting graphic scenes from epic battles between the forces of light and those of darkness. Demons, abominations, some winged and airborne, with features resembling the likes of frogs, many-headed dragons, snakes and other devils, were torturing and slaying apparent angels, decapitating them, impaling them, violating them. Some of the devils were horned and others even had faces on their backsides.

In the centre of the room was an altar, a table covered in the same silken, black, symbol-laden material that was used for the curtains in the other rooms. On the altar were two human skulls circled by ignited black candles and in the centre was a large, very sharp, exquisite dagger.

Mark was dazed by everything in front of his eyes - enchanted even - with the aroma of the sweet-smelling fumes from the fire filling his nose, lungs and head, dizzying him greatly before soon passing out. The last thing he saw before collapsing was a huge dark green snake darting at him from under the altar table and biting him on the right ankle. Then everything in his head faded to darkness...

***

When Mark regained consciousness he awoke in the same Satanic room. Everything was the same as it had been before, but the snake was nowhere to be seen. He had no idea how long he had been passed out for. His throat was dry and he stumbled as he tried to stand up. The weird, though pleasant aroma was even stronger in the room now. It seemed to ease and calm him somewhat. He was now feeling a little outside of himself, his senses fully heightened, fully aware of everything around him and in the room. It felt good, almost sexual even. He believed he could see strange, irregular shapes jumping out at him from the darkness, shapes with faces intent on malevolence, but for some reason he was no longer afraid. He welcomed them, in fact, and laughed maniacally to himself. These alien sensations, feelings and visions grew and grew, until reaching a fever pitch so intense Mark thought he might explode.

He lost his mind completely around this point, his sanity slipping away like a fish escaping a net.

The frenzied and hypnotised Mark Tate walked calmly over to the Satanic altar and lifted the ceremonial dagger in his best hand, the right one. He tilted his head back slowly, exposing his raw throat, and raised the blade before slamming it into his windpipe, his trachea, and played around inside of it for a bit before collapsing on the floor once again, deep crimson spurting and flowing from his gaping wound. As he lay on the ground with his life force ebbing rapidly away, Mark's thoughts turned briefly to the pleasant sight of the horses he had seen playing in the field earlier and then finally to terror and deep regret. Then it was all over for him in this world.

***

The Soul Devourer arrived at the house soon after to claim its reward from the Cruel and Forbidden Ones. It was still dressed elegantly in its red ceremonial robes and cloak, with its goat's head mask covering its diabolical, otherworldly facial features. Its immediate superiors had once again laid a trap for an unsuspecting member of the human race, who had fallen for it hook, line and sinker. The deception was now complete and the fresh soul was ready for harvesting by the cloaked entity standing in front of the now lifeless body.

Mark Tate's soul would soon be feasted upon and then dragged to the nethermost depths of eternal darkness and never-ending torment.

His second death was imminent.

LA MUERTE DE LA HUMANIDAD

'This is the coastal town,
They forgot to close down.
Armageddon, come Armageddon!
Come, Armageddon! Come!'
(Morrissey)

I once heard a quote in a war film that Hell is the impossibility of reason. I disagree. For me, Hell is many things, one of them being alone and afraid somewhere alien.

I was dreaming again.

This prison filled me full of dread. I didn't even know where it was, or by extension, where I was. It was somewhere foreign and hot, that's all I knew. Maybe it was Hell?

You could almost physically feel the atmosphere it was so tense. This was not a place of low level, petty criminals. No, this was where the hardcore of rapists and murderers resided and a riot was breaking out.

The four internal sides of the seemingly never ending caged floors and cells were alive with a bustling chaos. Madness was ensuing. Prisoners fought viciously with wardens and each other. Some of them were stabbing at their jailers with makeshift weapons made out of toothbrushes and razor blades. I saw a prisoner slash directly across the face of an officer, crimson spurting from his gaping wound, disfigured for life if he even managed to escape this horror show with his life intact. Fierce dogs were accompanying the wardens, bloodthirsty saliva dripping from their angry, hugely-toothed, mouths, hungry for some human meat. A muscular, tattooed and pony-tailed prisoner managed to break through an area of the caging surrounding the corridors and inexplicably leapt to his death, crushing onto the floor in a crunching heap of bone and flesh.

The insanity continued for what seemed like a very long time. Punchings. Kickings. Stabbings. Bitings. Heads being jumped upon. Limbs being removed. The whole place awash with blood and sinew. Debased. Humanity at its very worst. Such a violent species.

I left my cell and struggled through the sea of bodies attacking one another, eventually making it safely to the gym a few floors below. My only friend there, I think his name was Aaron, appeared and grabbed my hand, hastily demanding that I come with him as he knew where we must go to escape this nightmare completely.

We ran and made it outside to the prison yard. Away from the carnage but still within the grey walls of this wretched place. What was to follow was somewhat muddled. Vague even.

A river appeared in the yard and to reach the exit on the other side we had to cross it, like Charon himself making passage to the Ancient Greek Otherworld. Spare a coin for the ferryman, would you?

But before crossing the river, we made and ate some toast.

As we waded through the water, fanged unusual fish jumped from the water and attempted to sink their sharp teeth into us. Aaron continued to hold on to my hand tightly as we struggled across, our movements tediously slow, wading heavily forward as the weird fish bit at us, breaking the flesh somewhat and causing the river below to be partially dyed red.

At last, we made it to the other side, through the exit door and into the beautiful sunshine and daylight of the outside world. We stole a bright red convertible Porsche that had belonged to one of the presumably now butchered wardens and sped off into the countryside and freedom...

***

Merging seamlessly with with what had gone before, I now found myself alone in a desolate wasteland.

Buildings reduced to rubble. Broken glass everywhere. Mess. Houses destroyed. The aftermath of some cataclysmic event. Society as we know it no longer existing. Ghost town. A chilling, deafening silence.

I trudged through the debris all around me. A naked child's doll stared at me from the ground with its only remaining eye, it covered in dirt, its hair singed. The doll's right hand was pointing to the ruined remains of what used to be family homes straight in front of me. I walked towards them. The sky above was on fire, all shades of dark oranges and vivid reds, combusting turbulently. The sun no longer hung in the heavens, only this terrifying, menacing, flaming, carmine skyscape. I had a knowing feeling of great trepidation deep within the very pit of my stomach. Something really bad had happened. Something irreversible. Something final.

A lone church bell sounded in the distance.

I entered the first derelict house. It was awash with dust and the remnants of what used to be a happy home - the charred remains of electrical appliances, pictures that once hung proudly on walls, a burnt out sofa, children's toys and hand held computer games. All mod-cons now rendered completely useless and irrelevant.

A group of cockroaches in the soot-filled corner scuttled over each other, making unsettling clicking noises all the while. I entered a dining room. On what was left of a large oval dinner table sat a lone bird, staring at and through me with intentional malevolence, knowingly, its one visible large eye completely black as the darkest of dark nights. As it spread it wings magnificently, I realised it was a seagull and a massive one at that. Its wingspan and magnitude made it appear like an epic bird of prey, or perhaps even a pterodactyl. It was sporting a black eye patch on the left side of its face and on its beak rested an upward pointing Dali-esque moustache. Before it took flight, flying regally out of the glassless back window of the room, it squawked a message at me in a shrill, unearthly human tongue - "LA MUERTE DE LA HUMANIDAD!"

The ghosts then screamed out and spoke to me, relaying exactly what had happened.

The death of humanity had been a rather accelerated, nimble occurrence. No one seemed to know which country started the war or sent the nuclear missiles in the first place. Whichever madman pushed the button first was a mystery. It didn't matter in the end. When the people realised the terrible truth of what was going on there was a great screaming and weeping, wailing and gnawing of teeth. Amid the pandemonium and confusion, doomed souls rushed to be with their loved ones, bidding hysterical farewells as the afterlife beckoned for all. Vain, futile prayers were muttered.

But maybe this is what humanity really deserved after centuries of causing untold suffering and destruction everywhere it went. A collective suicide not caused by any god or cosmic being, but at the species' very own hand. There was something ironic about it. Perhaps Aldous Huxley was right after all. Maybe this world really was another planet's Hell.

Regardless, that day in the land of gods and monsters the human race went extinct not to prideful heroics, but to a grovelling, pathetic blubbering.

This was my final dream.

THE MIDNIGHT CHIMES

In total there are twelve Kings of Hell, also known as the Cruel and Forbidden Ones. In Hell, every denizen and soul which resides there - and they are countless - is subservient to these Kings, although there are some more esteemed subordinates than what you would find amongst the regular damned souls, if you pardon the expression. A couple of examples of these lesser demons directly under the command of the twelve Kings would be Ubu Mephistopheles, Herne the Hunter and Mr Needlesticks, mischievous malignant spirits whom often operate between the worlds on differing plains of existence altogether. But no being whatsoever is above the twelve Kings, whose rule is absolute and final. They have always ruled and they always will. The names of the twelve Kings of Hell are as follows: Astaroth, Maggot, Asmodee, Beelzebub, Oriens, Paimon, Ariton, Amaymon, Lucifer, Leviathan, Satan and Belial.

Every ten thousand years, for their own amusement, the Kings allow certain randomly selected souls of the damned to partake in a challenge, a game of sorts, with the prize for the victor a passageway back into the world of humankind, but under certain strict conditions, of course. It is believed, however, that no soul has ever completed the challenge and in fact the Kings are merely toying and tormenting those chosen for their own sadistic pleasures. The failure to succeed in the task at hand is met with the severest of punishments, as the unsuccessful ones are cast down into the furthest reaches of the Pit, imprisoned in the Ninth Circle, for a period of a four billion years, going by the Earthly time frame. It is in this Ninth Circle that the wailing and gnashing of teeth is at its most unrelenting, a region usually reserved for the most treacherous sinners of them all, their many aeons there spent frozen in the iciest of great lakes.

The terms of the game are simple and are as follows:

To qualify for the main arena each soul must solve the relatively difficult riddle of the Kings, which changes from game to game. The most recent riddle was the following:

> *They follow and lead, but only as you pass.*
> *Dress yourself in darkest black,*
> *And they are darker still.*
> *Always they flee the light,*
> *Though without the sun there would be none.*

All souls failing at the first hurdle of the riddle are, of course, cast down into the Ninth Circle, as previously stated. If the riddle is solved then the next stage for the competing soul or souls is to progress to the main event on the fields of Baal-Berith. Competitors are taken to the fields by the ancient ferryman, Ravana, across the filthy river of blood known as the Orusula.

The surroundings of the fields of Baal-Berith are consumed by the most beautiful and tragic chorus imaginable - the song of the Morfran - odd, unpleasant-looking creatures, with the distinctive look of a cricket fused with a frog. The Morfran are believed to have once been human beings before an ancient curse and punishment took a hold of them. Their unforgettable, operatic hymn is everlasting in its eeriness as it haunts the entire region.

On the dark fields of Baal-Berith, the final simplistic segment in the lottery of the lesser gods is taken. Those souls who have made it to this end game must progress alone across the devastatingly unholy plains on a journey that can take them, once again in human terms, one thousand, nine hundred and seventy-six years, all the while pursued relentlessly by the unspeakable hordes of the Jilayia, the abominations, the aborted offspring of demons and witches. The ultimate goal is to make it to the other side of the fields and the unholy palace of the Kings of Hell, known as Nimue, wherein these Cruel and Forbidden Ones are seated on their thrones in full wicked splendour. There, every few millennia, the magnificent centrepiece grandfather clock at their reverse altar of misery strikes midnight. Any successful competitor - and there has been none yet - must make it to the grandiose palace before the chimes of midnight. Once again, all competing souls who fail are banished to the nether regions of the Ninth Circle.

These are just some of the delights in store for those wretched, pitiful beings experiencing the second and final death.

I AM THE WAY TO THE CITY OF WOE, I AM THE BRINGER OF ETERNAL PAIN

'Better to reign in Hell than serve in Heaven.'
(John Milton, *Paradise Lost*)

Friday 21st December 2018, 7.34pm

"Who are you?" asked the psychiatrist seated behind his old wooden desk which had seen better days.

"I am no one. Who are you?" replied the gaunt, bald man with bony features and dark eyes sunken deep into their sockets sitting on the other side of the desk. He was wearing ill-fitting jeans and a white t-shirt which the hospital had supplied him with.

"I'm Doctor Chambers. I work at this facility, trying to help the patients here, treating their psychological and mental health issues through a combination of therapy and medication. At very least I hope I can help them live and deal with their conditions a bit more. It's not easy. But my main concern at the moment is your good self. I need to know who you are and how you came to be in this amnesic state you now find yourself in."

"I am no one," retorted the odd man with the strange, unidentifiable, though somewhat eloquent accent.

"So you say, but you must be someone. Can you remember any family or friends that I can contact to help you?"

A long, silent pause. The man studied the doctor's desk which had a small, poorly decorated Christmas tree on it, just beside the framed photograph of him with his wife and two young sons. With their jet black curling locks the boys resembled their father, much more so than their strawberry blonde, freckled mother. The picture had been taken outdoors, during some sort of holiday somewhere hot and pleasant with a beach. All smiles, they seemed to be a very happy, loving clan. At least in the photo anyway. Various other papers and clutter littered the rest of the unkempt desk. Eventually the man spoke again:

"Aaaahhhh, now that you mention it, I do seem to recollect having a mother and sisters at one time. But it was such a long time ago that I cannot for the life of me recall their names. I do apologise sincerely. It is all so very vague right now. It's been quite a while since I laid eyes upon them. Centuries really.'

"Are you trying to tell me you're hundreds of years old?" the doctor quipped with a smirk.

"Maybe. Perhaps. It's very cloudy. What is my diagnosis, Doctor Chambers?"

"It's hard to tell at this early stage. You are most certainly suffering from some sort of memory loss, brought on by a severe trauma of an unknown description. You were admitted to our care late last night. Do you know where you are exactly?"

"A hospital, I believe."

"That's correct. You're at the Lanchester Road psychiatric hospital in County Durham, England."

"How did I arrive in England? Last I remember I was in Northern Ireland. This is all very puzzling to me."

"Are you not from England? I can't seem to pin down your

accent. You don't sound Irish. Do you know where you are originally from? It might help us find out who you are."

"Who brought me to this hospital?"

"The police. You were found face down on an old cinder football pitch in a park, naked. A woman out walking her dog found you, believing you were drunk because of your incoherent mumblings. The cops couldn't identify you after doing various checks. Your fingerprints are not on their database, so you're not a known criminal to them. Your DNA was inconclusive also. They brought you to us because of your obvious mentally deteriorated state. We're just trying to help you here. You're not in any trouble with the law or anything. You're haven't been violent, or even aggressive in the slightest, just profoundly confused. You have nothing to worry about, I promise you."

"Why was the woman walking her dog? Could it not walk by itself?"

"I beg your pardon?"

Doctor Chambers lifted his pen off the desk and placed the end of it in his mouth. He'd been off the cigarettes for a couple of years and this was one of the ways he would keep his hands busy and replace the habitual part of the addiction in the early days. He hadn't done it in quite some time, but there was something about this patient that made him feel uneasy.

"Never mind. I don't think it's important," responded the confused man quietly, shaking his head.

The doctor put his pen back on the desk. "Do you know what day it is, or even the year?"

The patient thought for a while. "Is it 1985?"

"No, it's not," replied the doctor sternly, now becoming

somewhat rather impatient with the man, whom he now reckoned could be playing games with him and most probably concealing something of importance. "It's 2018, almost Christmas."

"That is very interesting indeed. I have been away for much longer than usual this time." retorted the man with a smile and a wave of his near skeletal right hand.

Doctor Chambers leaned in and looked closely at the man and his weird mannerisms. "Are you telling this has happened to you before?"

"I believe so, doctor."

"Compared to the state you were in last night, you do seem to have improved slightly. I don't think you've slept much, but at least you're talking sense now. Well, structured sentences anyway. Are things becoming a little clearer for you at all?"

The patient smiled eerily. "I believe I was imprisoned in a very bad place for many years."

"Since 1985 I suppose?"

"Correct."

"Why were you imprisoned? What did you do?"

"Disobeying my masters. Rebelling. Getting out of control."

"Who are your masters?"

"I cannot tell you that. It is forbidden. Are you recording our conversation?"

"No, I'm not. This is just a casual introductory chat. Would you like me to?"

"No, I wouldn't." The man pointed a bony finger to something on the desk. "What is that thing?"

"Oh, that? That's just my mobile."

"A mobile telephone?"

"Yes. Are you trying to tell me you've never seen or heard of mobile phones before?"

"I'm not sure."

"Where were you imprisoned? Where was this jail you speak of?"

"I believe I was imprisoned in a mirror, a dark place, a reverse world. I'd been there before, several times in fact."

"I find that hard to believe."

"That's understandable. It's an unbelievable story."

"Going back to your masters, what exactly did you do to disobey them?"

"I tried to overthrow one of them and take my rightful place at the others' side. I had earned a more elevated position. I deserved it and still do."

"What are you going to do about it then?"

"I don't know yet and even if I did I wouldn't tell you," stated the patient whilst winking at the doctor.

"Are you going to harm them or yourself in any way?"

"Not at all, doctor, I wouldn't harm a fly. By the way, doc, do you like magic?"

"What do you mean by 'magic'?"

"Stage magic, sleight of hand, Harry Houdini, those sorts of things."

"Oh, that sort of magic. Not really. That kind of thing never really appealed to me. My boys are big into Harry Potter though. That's them in the photo. Great kids, very imaginative."

"Who's Harry Potter?"

"It doesn't matter."

"I love magic. The unexpected. The suspense before the big reveal. Shocking, thrilling, surprising the audience. I'm such a show off. You don't happen to have a deck of cards on you, do you, doc?"

"No, I don't, sorry. So you're an amateur magician then."

"Professional."

"Sorry, professional."

Doctor Chambers was gradually finding this weird man quite unsettling, feeling more and more uncomfortable in his presence. There were so many things about him that didn't quite add up. He was thankful his office door was unlocked and the knowledge of those couple of burly male psychiatric nurses in the corridor outside made him feel a bit more at ease, however. He continued:

"The police tell me you androgynous, intersexual for want of a better word. How does that make you feel?"

The man smiled again. "It is of little to no importance. Irrelevant really."

Chambers placed his pen in his mouth again. The patient watched him carefully before asking:

"Are you performing that irritating ritual to stop yourself from smoking? If you really want to smoke you should just do it. It's not that bad of a habit anyway. There are much worse addictions, you know. We're all going to die of something one day, so you might as well make your short time on this world as pleasurable as possible."

The doctor removed the pen from his mouth and returned it to the desk. This man was perturbing him even more so now. "Not short for you though, friend, as you have lived for centuries. Or so you say."

"Yes, indeed. I am almost three hundred years old."

"Are you a time traveller?"

"No, of course not. That would be preposterous. Such a silly question."

"Is that so? You seem much better now, with your memory seemingly returning somewhat. Can you remember your name yet?"

"I'm Jack the Ripper," the man offered casually.

The doctor responded with a nervous sarcasm, "Well, of course you are, what with being centuries old and so forth."

"That was such a fun time. Gutting those awful whores from Whitechapel like mere fish."

"I don't believe you."

"It is of no relevance whatsoever what you believe. By the way, am I under some sort of arrest? I believe you stated that I was not under any investigation by the police. Am I free to go?"

"You were brought here for your own well being, very mentally distressed. Technically I could sign a few forms which would ensure you were legally turned over to our care, sectioned, for want of a better phrase. We would then monitor you for a few weeks. But as you have shown significant progress in your recovery already, I don't see the point. You haven't shown any signs of aggressive behaviour to anyone, so there is no real evidence to say that you are an immediate danger to yourself or anyone else. This is why you were admitted to ourselves at this low security wing of the hospital in the first place. There are obvious issues need addressing with you, however, no more so than the question of your identity and where you will go to stay. You still don't seem to be in touch with reality so that therefore makes you vulnerable to me. We're not just going to kick you out onto the street. You don't even appear to have any money. You're quite the conundrum, friend. What about this mother and sisters you spoke of, can you recall anyone at all?"

A pause.

"I'm sorry. I can't help you, doctor."

"In that case I'm going to have to recommend you stay in our care for a couple of weeks, at least until we can properly access you and get to the bottom of who you actually are and where you're from. Voluntarily, of course. We're here to help."

Another pause, this time more elongated and tense.

With an unexpected velocity and stamina, the man suddenly pounced onto the desk, grabbing the doctor by his greying black curls, pulling back his head in a tightened grip. Chambers gasped in shock while his patient reached over and secured the snib on the lock of the office door with his free hand and then grabbed the doctor's stylish pen. The man pushed his face directly in front of Chambers' terrified countenance and smiled with a gleeful menace, his eyes now turned completely black, before speaking in a slow, soft, yet highly threatening manner in his unusual Franco-esque accent:

"My name...is...Ubu Mephistopheles. My masters' names are the Cruel and Forbidden Ones. Welcome to my horror show, you stupid, insignificant fuck!"

Ubu Mephistopheles, former sinister circus clown, violently lunged the good doctor's fancy pen, which he had at one time used to help him quit smoking, deep into his exposed throat. Dark red liquid spurted from the wound, including over Ubu's face and t-shirt, as a wide-eyed Chambers gargled and tried to speak, but to avail as his life quickly ebbed from him, soon dropping his head in eternal silence.

Ubu quickly jumped off the desk and got down on his knees on the office floor, his eyes still as black as the darkest of shadows, and let out a shrill, deafening animalistic howl, as two small apparent horns appeared on his bald head.

By the time the large muscular psychiatric nurses from the corridor had broken down the door, obviously alerted by all the commotion, the doctor's odd patient had already escaped through the office window, smashing it with a fire extinguisher. When the police arrived a short while later, it was also a case of too little, too late, their suspect having fled through the surrounding grass banks and trees, long gone into the night. A large manhunt followed over the weekend, with the general public alerted to the extremely dangerous individual now at large, but alas, it would prove to be fruitless.

Suffice to say, Ubu Mephistopheles was now back in the world of living souls with some unfinished business to attend to...

The series will be concluded in...

PHANTASMAGORIA Book 3: MY JERUSALEM

'May you dream of lovely things and wake to find them real.'
(JJ Heller)

ABOUT THE AUTHOR

Trevor Kennedy is a writer and editor based in Belfast, Northern Ireland, and creator of the *Phantasmagoria* horror series. He also produces the *Gruesome Grotesques* anthology book series and *Phantasmagoria Magazine*. In the past, he was a regular contributor for *FEAR Magazine* and has also contributed stories for several anthologies, including: *The Thirteen Signs, Floppy Shoes Apocalypse 2* and *3, Chunks: A Barfzarro Anthology,* and *Slashing Through the Snow: A Christmas Horror Anthology*.

Upcoming works include *Phantasmagoria III: My Jerusalem,* and his first novel, *Time Travel for Junkies: A Beginner's Guide*.

Trevor is also a presenter for Big Hits Radio UK and actor. He can be contacted at tkboss@hotmail.com.

Printed in Poland
by Amazon Fulfillment
Poland Sp. z o.o., Wrocław